TO SADDLE
A DREAM

TO SADDLE
A DREAM

•

Frances Engle Wilson

AVALON BOOKS
NEW YORK

PRINTED IN THE UNITED STATES OF AMERICA
ON ACID-FREE PAPER
BY HADDON CRAFTSMEN, BLOOMSBURG, PENNSYLVANIA

To my dear friend, Zelda Adams,
whose lovely name I borrowed for my heroine.

"All that we see or seem,
Is but a dream within a dream."
—Edgar Allan Poe

My grateful thanks to Martha Edson, who knows horses like the back of her hand, and shared her knowledge and know-how with me.

And to Bill Tackett, breeder and trainer of race horses, for his interest, generous help, and invaluable information.

Chapter One

"**W**hat do you mean my name isn't on your list? And since when does a person need an invitation to get into an estate sale anyway? Tyler Wakefield's warm, southern voice was beginning to have a caustic edge to it. "This Nathan Redmond sale was advertised in the Lexington newspaper this morning, and the way I see it that means it's open to the public," he drawled with distinct mockery.

"I know that, but the public sale begins tomorrow. Today is the pre-sale. The Redmond family requested this. With someone as well known as Nathan Cyrus Redmond was, they feel his friends and banking associates should be given an opportunity to select things before the

1

antique and art collectors and the public come in." Zelda explained carefully, maintaining her most courteous and professional manner. After all, Iverson's had the finest reputation for handling estate and consignment sales of anyone in the business; not only in the state of Kentucky, but throughout the entire South. Zelda knew all too well that her father, Claude Iverson, had earned this not only because he was in the International Society of Appraisers, but because of his artful finesse in dealing with people. At this moment she could only wish that he were here to smooth over this present situation. "I'm sorry, but today's pre-sale is private, Mr. Wakeford. Please understand that only those whose names are on my list can attend," she continued, offering him what she hoped was a gracious smile.

"Field—not Ford. Wakefield is my name. And, as a matter of fact I knew Nathan Redmond for a good many years. He was a kind and generous friend to me and my family. So maybe you could check that list of yours again for the name Wakefield." He spoke with quiet firmness, then waited, challenging her to do it.

She glanced down at the clipboard she held in her hand, a suggestion of annoyance hovering in her eyes. "The only W names are Wamsley, Whitney, Wilson, and Wright," she said. "Here, see for yourself." She held the list out where he could see it. "I'm afraid you'll just have to come back tomorrow. I assure you you'll be most welcome then."

Tyler's expression was clouded in frustration. "Look, lady, I can't come to Lexington tomorrow. I've got a mare at my farm ready to foal. I took a risk to drive in today, and the only reason I did was because it's important to me to buy some small memento that belonged to Nathan Redmond. Don't you see, that fine, old gentleman was my benefactor. All I ask is that you give me fifteen minutes to go into the library and pick up a little keepsake—like one of his briar wood pipes, a paperweight, or a letter opener off his desk. Surely, you could allow me to do that. What possible harm could that do to anyone?" The expression in his hazel eyes seemed to plead for her understanding.

"I've explained why I can't allow that," she said, shaking her head. "Please try and understand." She sighed in exasperation. "It's my job to conduct this sale according to the wishes of the family. There can be no exceptions. If your name is not on the list, then you can't come in." She stepped back, making a move to close the the door.

"Wait!" Tyler held out his hand to stop her. "I just thought of something you could do that could solve this whole problem for both of us.

Nathan's daughter, Rosalind, knows me very well. If you'll just ask her about me, I know she'll add my name to that list of yours. Her married name is Trask."

"I'm sorry, but Barton Redmond is the one who engaged Iverson's to handle his father's estate sale. He and his son Mathew stipulated the details of the pre-sale. His sister was not even mentioned as being here for it, as far as I know. It's our understanding that when she was here for her father's funeral she selected the things from the estate that she wanted and arranged for them to be shipped to her home. I believe she lives someplace in the Northwest. Is that right?"

"Yeah, she and her husband live in Seattle. Robert Trask is head of a large seafood-canning company." A disappointed grimace tightened his mouth. "Well, I've run out of arguments. So you win, lady," his mellow baritone voice was edged with control. "I don't like it, and you're sure a stickler for rules, but I guess that's the way it goes when a guy who's all heart runs up against a woman who's all business." There was a critical tone to his voice and a distinct hardening of his eyes. Then without waiting for her to reply, he spun around on his boot heels and left.

Irritated by his sarcasm and censure, Zelda stared after his retreating back. Her annoyance increased as she closed the front door and found that her hands were shaking. She clutched the clip board to her breast and marched off. She'd done the right thing. Actually, she'd done the only thing she could do. She certainly had no reason to feel guilty about it. Yet for some inexplicable reason, she did. She shook her head in exasperation. Glancing at her wristwatch, she realized she couldn't afford to be distracted further. It was time she started making her rounds through the main rooms of the house where the major pieces of furniture and the expensive art objects were displayed. A pre-sale of an estate like this one required that she and her father act like a hostess and host. Creating a rather partylike atmosphere made for a highly successful sale, particularly so because all the people here had been invited. They all enjoyed the special feeling of knowing that they were having the first choice of the beautiful furnishings that filled the many rooms of the late Nathan Redmond's historic, antebellum home.

Girding herself with resolve and placing a serene smile on her face, Zelda walked from the vestibule into the parlor where a dozen or so men and women were examining various oil paintings, and the antique Chippendale and Hepplewhite style furnishings.

Claude Iverson was standing in front of the fireplace, obviously discussing the fan shaped brass firescreen with an interesting looking middle-aged man with a gaunt but rather handsome face. When Zelda caught her father's eye, he moved his hand in a slight gesture to indicate he had everything in this room under control. She nodded her head to him, smiled, and strolled unhurriedly in the direction of the dining room.

Through what remained of the morning and for most of the afternoon, a sizeable group of people roamed through the Redmond house admiring its contents and purchasing quite a number of its treasures. At five o'clock, Claude Iverson locked the front door after the last customer with a gleam of satisfaction in his rounded blue eyes. With a few streaks of silver in his dark hair, Zelda's father was a tall, distinguished looking man in his midfifties.

Zelda had the best traits of both parents. She was slender like her mother, with what the fellow she dated her first year in college claimed were the greatest pair of legs in the state of Kentucky. Zelda figured this flattery was all part of his line, but she liked hearing it anyway. She had her dad's color of hair, but of course, there were no strands of silver in hers. Her hair was dark as a blackbird's wing, and her eyes were blue-violet like her third-generation Irish mother, whose name had been Kathleen O'Roark before she married Claude Maloney Iverson.

* * *

Barton Redmond had arrived at the house shortly before the sale ended for the day. He was now asking her father how he thought the pre-sale had gone. "Extremely well, I'd say," Claude replied. "Zelda can show you the inventory list, and the items with a check beside them are what sold today."

Zelda turned to leave the room. "I'll go get our notebook. It's with the cashier who was taking the money."

"No, stay here. I can look it over at another time," Barton assured her. "As I walked through a few of the rooms I could see some empty spaces on the walls and several pieces of furniture that I was used to seeing had disappeared. It looks like the sale got off to a good start." Barton bestowed a condescending smile on Zelda. "Would you say most of the folks on the list turned up?"

Zelda nodded. "Ninety percent of them did. I'd be willing to bet on that." She matched her bright tone with her smile. "Wouldn't you agree with that Dad?"

He nodded. "It was one of our more successful pre-sales, I'll say that. Lots of interest has been generated. I anticipate a record turnout when we open the sale to the public tomorrow morning."

"And speaking of highly interested people,

there was an eager man today whose name was not on your list. He was very persistent and insisted that he be allowed to come in. He claimed your father had befriended his family. I had some difficulty getting him to leave," Zelda explained.

"Who was he?" Barton asked.

"He said his name was Wakefield."

"Oh yes—Tyler Wakefield. I might have guessed he'd show up here."

"He claimed that your sister would have seen to it that his name be on the list. Nevertheless, I told him he'd have to come back for the public sale."

"Well, he's probably right about Rosalind. My sister is sentimental to a point of being maudlin," Barton scoffed, and his pale eyes became flat and unreadable as stone. He turned his attention again to Zelda's father. "I must say, Iverson, you and your crew have gotten this affair started off in fine style. I'm sure the public sale will go equally well." Having said this, the portly banker buttoned the coat of his sedate gray suit and left.

Zelda watched him leave, a puzzled frown puckering the bridge of her nose. Barton Redmond certainly wasn't a particularly friendly or ingratiating sort of man. At least, she didn't find him so. She was curious though about his reaction when she told him about Wakefield wanting to be allowed to attend the pre-sale today. Apparently there was some past history between the Redmonds and Wakefield that didn't sit too well with Barton. However, it would seem his sister's opinion of Wakefield differed greatly from his. For Barton to characterize his sister as sentimental, even maudlin, in such a scathing tone showed he felt a bit of contempt for Tyler Wakefield, and possibly for Rosalind as well. But why? What had happened between the two families? Was it some kind of a feud? Whatever his reason, the banker seemed to resent the younger man's interest in attending the sale. She narrowed her eyes in speculation. If Rosalind Trask had been here today, it would have made for an interesting scenario. Too bad she wasn't, Zelda thought. It intrigued her to consider what might have happened if Barton's sister had been available to add Tyler Wakefield's name to the pre-sale list.

"Do come along now, Zelda," her father's crisp voice broke into her thoughts. "Let's not waste any more time. We've got to straighten things up to be ready for tomorrow. You know the dealers will be here well before nine to be first in line. The security guards will arrive by eight-fifteen, and I'll need you here by then too. The first day of a public sale means a crowd crush right from the start."

"Yes Dad," she breathed a weary sigh. "I

know that all too well." She quickly joined him. "So let's make a speedy job of this and get out of here.

For the following three days, Zelda's every moment was involved with the estate sale. As they had anticipated, people from all around the Lexington area came in droves to browse through the rooms of the Redmond house, admire the contents, and buy, and buy. So now, at closing time on the third and final day, the house was practically sold down to the bare walls. It was another highly successful Iverson estate sale.

Shortly before five o'clock, Bargain Ben, the thrift store dealer made his usual appearance to check out the remaining mishmash of china, glass, kitchenware and the well-worn divan, and three or four other pieces of nondescript furniture that hadn't sold. While her father and the shrewd Bargain Ben huddled in the dining room to come to an agreement on the meager amount the canny dealer would pay for what was left, Zelda went upstairs to check out the rooms and make sure everyone but the Iverson's work crew had left. As she started back down the stairs, the front door swung open.

"Hey, I'm just getting in under the wire I bet." A man's hearty voice boomed out, echoing along the now barren walls of the vestibule. "I know

I'm late, but please don't tell me I can't come in this time."

Zelda had reached the first floor and now stood at the bottom of the stairs resting one hand on the balustrade. "You're already in, and I welcome you, Mr. Wake*field*," she said, a smile in her voice as she exaggerated the last part of his name, emphasizing the fact that she had stated it correctly this time. "I guess your mare must have finally had her foal. Right?"

"Right—at two-thirty this morning to be precise. And a splendid, thoroughbred colt he is too," Tyler declared, with a beaming smile that spread across his deeply tanned face. Exposure to the sun had also given a bronze glint to his light brown hair.

He was certainly pleasant looking when he smiled, Zelda thought. She hadn't been aware that he was quite so tall and broad shouldered before either. The other day she'd only noticed that he had a firm, stubborn jaw, and she'd found him rather irritating, to say the least. Today, however, he seemed rather charming.

"I'd say your day got off to an exciting start. I only wish I could keep it from ending on a down note. But I'm afraid that you've come back too late. Everything has been sold. Honestly, there's nothing of real significance or value left in this house. I'm really sorry."

Disppointment altered his expression. "It doesn't have to be much, you know. Surely there's some small memento I can salvage."

"Well there are some books left in the library that we were about to relegate to the thrift store dealer. You can look through those if you like."

"Yeah, show them to me." He walked over to join her.

Zelda turned away from the stairs and lead the way through the empty front areas of the house and into Nathan Redmond's study. The dark, richly detailed cherry paneling and the massive, hand-carved mantle gave the impressive library a very masculine feel.

There were some thirty or forty books still strewn along the library shelves. Tyler immediately began sorting through them, taking one down at a time to leaf through it.

"The majority of these books seems to relate to economics and financial planning," he remarked as he replaced one he'd examined back on the shelf. "I would think that Barton would be interested in putting some of the more current ones in his office at the bank."

"Evidently not. He looked over everything that remained in the house this morning and told me there was nothing he wanted to salvage. He doesn't strike me as having much family sentiment. His orders were that whatever remained at five o'clock when the sale ended was to be turned over to a second-hand dealer."

Tyler shrugged. "Barton is a bit of a cold fish, and he's totally self-seeking. In no way is he the kind of man his father was. The only thing Nathan and Barton shared is the Redmond name."

For a second Tyler looked like he was going to say something further. Then he must have decided against it because he looked away from Zelda and then stooped down to gaze into the cabinets that were underneath the book shelves.

"Well, what do you know!" Tyler exclaimed, a jubilant sound in his voice and a wide grin spreading across his face. "Talk about warm sentiments and family ties! Nathan kept this through the years." He held up a curved piece of rusted iron.

"Why that's an old, rusty horseshoe, isn't it?"

Tyler chuckled. "You bet it is. And how well I remember that August day when Sweet Dream threw this shoe. Sara got so excited, and she asked me to let her have it so she'd have something of Sweet Dream's to keep with her when she couldn't be with her horse." Tyler's expression stilled and grew serious. "It was that last summer that she spent in Kentucky with the Redmonds—a special time for Sara and Nathan. It's no wonder that he would have kept this." There was a note of nostalgia in Tyler's voice as he said this. Then he glanced down again at the horseshoe he still held in his hand. "I'd like to buy this," he said, bending over to look at the rest of the contents of the cardboard box. "In fact, I want this whole box of stuff that was with the horseshoe. What's the price on it?"

Nonplussed by his request, Zelda tossed her hands up not knowing what to say. "Honestly, it's just some newspaper clippings, and a few old letters, and photographs that came from the bottom drawer of the desk. Barton labeled it clutter and told Dad to just toss it out as worthless trash."

"Well it's worth something to me," he said, straightening up and pulling his wallet from his hip pocket. "Would ten dollars be about right?" he asked.

"I'd say that's more than generous," she said, shaking her head at him. "I have to admit though that I'm surprised that you want such stuff as this." She paused, shrugging her shoulders. "But I guess from what you've told me, this horseshoe and probably the other things in that box will have meaning for you."

"Yes, I think so. I'm very glad to have found it, and I really thank you for bearing with me." He smiled, eyeing her thoughtfully. "Incidently, my first name is Tyler, and I'd like to know your name if you don't mind telling me."

She smiled. "I don't mind at all. It's Iverson—Zelda Iverson."

"Zelda—I've never heard that name before. I like the sound of it. It's lyrical."

Having said this, Tyler picked up the box he'd bought and started to leave the room. At the library door he stopped, momentarily, looked back over his shoulder and said. "I shall remember you, Zelda."

She remained motionless in the center of the room after he'd gone. She'd never had anyone comment about her name before. It left her in a quandary. She didn't know what to make of Tyler's unusual and rather charming remarks. If it was a line he used to catch the interest of each new woman he met, at least it was original. She would have to give him that.

She smiled inwardly while thinking Tyler Wakefield was certainly not the sort of man you meet everyday. It intrigued her that he had been so happy to discover that rusted horseshoe. It just proved that old cliché that one man's trash is another man's treasure. Certainly these past forty-five minutes that she'd spent with this surprising man had raised some questions in her mind. One in particular she thought, arching an eyebrow curiously. Who was this Sara that Tyler had talked about? And where did she fit into the Redmond-Wakefield equation, she wondered.

Chapter Two

Organizing a successful estate sale is a time-consuming business. For the Nathan Redmond sale, Zelda and her father spent eight hours a day for two weeks prior to the actual sale to inventory the contents of the house and price each item. This also required research on Claude's part to appraise the value of Redmond's antiques, art work, and in particular, Nathan's extensive and valuable stamp collection. Needless to say, Zelda welcomed the news when her father told her that they would not start an inventory for the next sale before the middle of April. Happily that date was nearly a month away.

For a pleasant change of pace, Zelda planned to spend this time meeting with the clients who wanted Iverson's to take their things for sale on consignment. Zelda enjoyed doing this. It often proved interesting, and sometimes entertaining because of the quaint and strange objects some people wanted her to sell for them. Once in a while she was even told personal and touching reasons that the clients had for needing to sell their special treasures.

This particular March afternoon, there was a smell of spring in the still cool earth. Here and there some bulbs were thrusting up shafts of green, and even the sounds of spring emanated from a passing robin, mockingbird, or a pausing pair of mourning doves.

Early that afternoon Zelda had driven out in the countryside to carry out some business with Philip and Linda Martin, an enterprising young couple who had recently acquired an early nineteenth-century plantation house. To Zelda, the house and it's setting surrounded by stately oak trees, was reminiscent of Tara in *Gone With The Wind*, only on a smaller scale.

Zelda's interest was captivated by the Martins' fascinating story of discovering a cachet of old treasures while they were in the process of re-modeling this house. Linda explained that one of the major alterations that needed to be made required moving the staircase a few feet to one side. In doing this, a hidden area was disclosed under the stairs. And stored away in this odd, triangular shaped space the Martins found two sizeable oil paintings, framed in impressive gilt frames. Also wrapped up in old horse blankets were several silver trays and a meat platter, a silver tea service, and two pairs of three branch candelabra. Last but not least the Martins unearthed a Confederate officer's sword hanging from a nail on the highest point of this peculiarly shaped enclosure. It was these items that Philip Martin was just now loading into the back of Zelda's van to be sold when Iverson's held their next auction sale.

"I'll get back to you in about a week when my father has the appraisals ready on your things. At that time we'll send the sales agreement for you to sign and return," Zelda said, as she opened the door and got in the van.

As she drove off she glanced at the clock on the dash-board and noted with dismay that it was already twenty past four. She let out a sigh, realizing she was at least twenty miles outside of Lexington and that meant she'd be hitting the city limits just at the height of the five o'clock rush hour. She hated to drive the company van in heavy traffic. It didn't maneuver easily like her own little Mazda. But, of course, when she was gathering up large items for Iverson consignment sales, it required her to drive the Iverson van. She simply shouldn't have lingered so long with Linda and Philip Martin. But, she defended herself with a quick toss of her head, she couldn't miss out on the intriguing tale about how the Martins found this valuable collection of items that dated back to the glory days of the Old South. Why, in Zelda's imagination, it even seemed highly possible that the paintings and the silver had been tucked away behind that staircase for more than a hundred years. More than likely, they were stashed in that secret place to keep from being confiscated by Yankee soldiers. She chuckled under her breath thinking that certainly could be the true story. And anyway, who was there to dispute her? She laughed gaily and accelerated.

Considering the fact that everybody would have left by the time she got back to the building, Zelda pulled the van off onto the next wide shoulder of the country road and let her motor idle as she reached for the car phone and quickly punched in the number. After just two rings, Carrie Lee's silky, southern voice announced, "Iverson's Sales, may I help you?"

"It's me, Carrie Lee. I'm running late and it'll be well after five before I get back. I know you'll be gone by then, and I wanted to check and see if you had any messages for me."

"Well, I should say there is," she drawled. "A

Tyler Wakefield has called twice. He said it's quite important that he talk to you. Something about a box he bought at the Redmond sale. He was very anxious about it, even insisted that I give him your home phone number." She paused long enough to heave a sigh. "I do hope I didn't do the wrong thing to give it to him. He just wasn't going to stop pestering me until I did. My word, he's a persistent one, isn't he?"

Zelda laughed. "You can say that again. He's not one to take no for an answer either, so it's okay about my number. I can't imagine that anything about that box he bought could be that important, but apparently he's going to tell me." Zelda laughed again.

Having completed the call, Zelda stowed away the car phone and eased the van back again onto the highway. As she drove, she continued to smile and think about the fact that Tyler had not only called the office twice, but had inveigled Zelda's home number out of Carrie Lee, the Miss Congeniality of the Iverson Sales Company. Either there really was something important about that box he bought, or he was using that as an excuse to talk to her again. It was an interesting scenario either way, and Zelda's curiosity, as well as her vanity, was aroused. She couldn't deny that she felt a spark of excitement at the possibility that this ruggedly handsome and thoroughly compelling man might be showing a bit of interest in her.

As she drove closer to Lexington the traffic grew heavier, but it was moving rapidly. Arriving at the building, she parked the van beside the rear door. She was relieved to see that her father's car was also still there. She gave the horn two short blasts which was their signal and in record time her dad came out to help her unload the van.

"Looks like you hauled in some interesting stuff," Claude commented.

"Yeah, and there's a fascinating story to go with these things too." She passed the sword to him over the back seat. "But I'll tell you all about it over breakfast. You did say you were going to your dinner bridge group tonight. Right?"

He nodded. "Big night too. I understand there's to be six tables, and possibly some new prospective members."

"They're probably recruiting some sharpies to try and take the club trophy away from you this year," she said, smiling at him. "So strut your stuff tonight, 'cause my money's staying on you, Dad."

Bridge had been her parents' favorite pastime throughout their thirty-two-year marriage. After her mother died a year and a half ago, her dad turned to bridge for solace. He not only got involved in a weekly bridge club, but also took every opportunity to join in a game on a moment's notice. So it wasn't unusual for him to be out two or three times a week. Zelda knew how much he enjoyed his bridge, but she sensed that he did this partly to make things easier on her. However, keeping house for her father was what she wanted to do, and furthermore, she enjoyed the comfort and security of living in the house where she'd grown up and spent all of her twenty eight years.

The Iverson house was in an attractive residential area of Lexington—a quiet haven where massive oaks and hickory trees shaded well-loved manors and charming cottages and where everyone knew everyone else. Her parents had bought this home the year before Zelda was born. They had chosen it because it inclined toward the uncontrived sophistication of an English country house. Also, the exterior, with its asymmetrical facade of weathered bricks gave it a look of age. Claude Iverson was often heard to say that he liked homes that look as if they've been lived in and loved for generations. His own home looked that way, as did so many of those in which he conducted estate sales. Obviously this was one of the main reasons he enjoyed his line of work so much, and continued being successful at it.

These thoughts were mingling around in Zelda's head after she left her father to lock up the van and drove to the house in her own car. In less than fifteen minutes she was swinging off the wide boulevard onto the narrower, tree-lined street where she lived.

Inside the house, the soft amber glow of a serene twilight was filtering through the western windows picking up the soft rose, blue, and yellow of the round Persian rug in the entry hall. She draped her jacket over the newel post at the base of the staircase and set her briefcase and purse on the bottom step ready to be carried upstairs later on. Then she marched immediately back to the kitchen, took a chicken and artichoke casserole out of the refrigerator, placed it in the oven and turned the dial to three hundred and fifty degrees. Her mundane chores done, she finally went to the phone and punched the button to hear her messages.

"Zelda, this is Tyler. I hear third time is the charm, and I've called you twice at your office and now at your house. Sure am anxious to talk to you. Phone me at any hour, early or late, but call me back soon." Tyler's message was loud and clear, and echoed that insistent tone of his. "Here are my two numbers—the first is my house—the second the stable. I'll be at one place or the other. It's important. Do call—please."

Amused and sort of flattered at his urgency, Zelda picked up the receiver and called his house. He answered so quickly, she thought he must have been sitting by the telephone just waiting for her to call.

"I just got home and heard your message," she told him. "I've been out driving around the countryside all afternoon on business."

"Yeah, that's what I finally found out from that young woman at your office. She's certainly chary with her information. I got the impression that she was leery of my motives. Figured I was chasing you down to complain about that box I bought at the sale."

"Well are you?—complaining, I mean."

"No way," he exclaimed staunchly. "You know better than that. The contents of that box interest me greatly. Besides, there's one item of some value that I want to return to you tomorrow evening if you're free for dinner. Are you?"

"Yes, as a matter of fact, I am."

"Good. I'll pick you up at six-thirty if that's okay. I like to get to the restaurant ahead of the crowd," he added, laughing. "I figure I get a better table that way and the rolls are hotter and the coffee is fresher."

His laugh was infectious and she answered in

an amused tone. "You make a good point, and six-thirty sounds like the ideal time to get a neat table and hot, tasty food."

"Well then, we're in total agreement on the time. Now let's talk about the place. I've got a friend who's a partner with his parents in a fairly new restaurant here in Lexington. It's a small place with a genuine Neapolitan atmosphere and the best veal rolled with prosciutti and cheese served with marinara sauce that you've ever tasted. I'm talking about Villa Vinelli. Do you go for Italian food, or would you rather stick to American prime and go to The Steak House? Think about it and you can tell me when I see you tomorrow night."

"I don't need to think about it, Tyler. I like the sound of your Villa Vinelli. And I love going to some place new and different," she said without a moment's hesitation.

"Way to go, Zelda!" Tyler exclaimed warmly. "I'm beginning to think that you and I may be on the same wave length after all."

The Villa Vinelli proved to be all that Tyler said it was and more. The interior was something like a nineteenth century church with light shining through stained glass. And in this charming setting, incredible Italian food was generously and attractively served. The atmosphere was warm and friendly, and there was the appealing fragrance of bread baking and the intriguing aroma of Italian wines and spices.

Light conversation flowed easily between Tyler and Zelda as they ate their dinner, but the subject of the Redmond sale was not brought up. Zelda began to suspect that Tyler had only used the ploy of having discovered something valuable in that box he purchased merely to get her to go out on a date with him. The idea amused her. From what she'd seen of Tyler Wakefield so far, he was hardly a man who employed subtle measures to get what he wanted.

"I'm wondering when you're going to get around to telling me what was valuable in that box of yours?" Zelda asked finally while they waited for their dessert to be served. "I thought that was the whole reason for our getting together tonight."

"No, not entirely," he said, letting his gaze travel over her in lazy appraisal. "I had another reason too."

She narrowed her eyes quizzically. "Oh, you did. And what was that?"

"Well, you were so totally all business at the sale, and I was curious to know if you were the same away from work as you are on the job." His eyes were very alive and filled with a strong intelligence that was now alertly studying her.

"And am I?"

"No—not entirely the same."

She bristled slightly. "And what does that mean exactly?"

"It means you're approachable without that clipboard in your hands," he said, giving her a placating smile. "I'm more comfortable sitting across the table from you here than I was standing outside the door at the Redmond sale."

She gave Tyler an arch look. "I'm glad a guy who's all heart finds some bit of saving grace in a gal who's all business."

"Oh I assure you, Zelda, I find much more than a mere bit," Tyler said, looking at her with more than mild interest.

His look was so galvanizing, it sent a tremor through her. She waited until her quickened pulse quieted before she returned to her original question. "Come on now, stop changing the subject and tell me what it is you found in that box with the horseshoe?"

"Here, I'll show you," he said, pulling an envelope from his pocket and handing it to her.

"You mean you found a letter that you think has some value to it?" She peered at the envelope curiously, noting that there was no name or address written on it.

"It's not a letter, Zelda. Open it."

She looked inside the envelope and removed

a packet wrapped in a sheet of letter paper. "Why, it's money," she exclaimed as she unfolded the paper.

"Yeah, twelve twenties, nine tens, and four fives to be exact."

"But that can't be. Barton told me he went through that box and there was nothing but old photos and letters that no one would want. He called it trash. Told me to throw it out." She stared at the bills in her hand, all the time shaking her head, a disturbed expression on her face. "It's my job to examine every item in an estate sale. I should have checked the contents of that carton myself. Something like this just isn't allowed to happen at an Iverson's sale." She heaved a ragged sigh.

"Well, it's not your fault. In fact it's not really Barton's either. It certainly appeared to be a box of ordinary stuff, plus a bunch of old personal letters that could be of no interest to anyone but Nathan. This envelope with the bills in it was mixed in with a dozen or more of similar size. Barton would have had to open each one and unfold each sheet of paper to discover this money. Barton could never be bothered with doing that."

"Nevertheless, I should have done exactly that." Zelda said, as she now scrutinized the envelope and the sheet of onion skin paper that was folded around the cash. "This envelope is not addressed to anyone, and the only thing written on this sheet of paper is *Thanks* followed by the letter *R*. You think R. is for Redmond?"

"Possibly. Or it could be R for Rosalind."

She frowned. "You think so?"

"Just a guess," he said, shrugging. "It could be that someone gave it to Nathan to repay a debt or a loan. At this late date it doesn't really matter where it came from, does it? You can just add it to the proceeds of the estate sale."

"Better yet, Tyler, you could give it to Barton. After all, you're the one who found it, you should get the credit."

"No way. I don't want credit and I won't do that. Furthermore, I don't care to have Barton know I had any part in it," he answered in a tense, clipped voice that forbade any questions.

Taken back by Tyler's stern expression, Zelda frowned, regarding him with a speculative gaze. "Since you feel that way, I'll take care of it then."

"Good. Believe me, that's best for all concerned."

Tyler's terse words put an end to any further discussion on this subject. Apparently Tyler's friendly relationship with Nathan Redmond and his daughter Rosalind did not extend to Barton.

Not that this surprised her, for she found Barton somewhat overbearing.

"You know, Tyler, I hope you found something of value to you in that box," she said, her dark eyebrows raised inquiringly. "I'm going to feel guilty if you paid ten dollars for nothing more than a rusty horseshoe."

"Believe me, I did. A pleased look brightened his eyes. "Hidden away under the letters and pictures was Nathan's ebony wood handled magnifying glass. I'd seen him peer through it lots of times when he was pouring over that stamp collection of his. It's exactly the sort of keepsake I was hoping for. And it's something of Nathan's that I'll keep on my desk at the farm and make good use of." There was a ring of satisfaction in his voice and the beginnings of a smile on his lips.

"That's great, Tyler. I'm glad you got something you truly wanted."

He nodded. "Yeah, and some of the pictures are special too."

"Hey, that's super. Tell me about them." Suddenly she became more animated. She actually had felt guilty about all of this, and it was a tremendous relief to learn that Tyler had gotten a desired memento of his benefactor. Now there was even more memorabilia to please him. She exhaled a sigh of contentment.

"Well, there are thirty or more snapshots of Sara and Nathan at the stables with Sweet Dream, and Sara riding her horse on a number of different occasions. In fact, it's a pictorial record of Sara's experiences learning to handle and ride her horse. It shows the joy she found because she got to realize her dream." There was a faint tremor in his voice as though some emotion had touched him. He paused for only a second, then quickly continued. "I need to ask a favor, Zelda. I want you to get Rosalind's address from the Redmonds so I can mail these photos to her."

Zelda looked puzzled. "But you said the pictures were all of Sara."

"He nodded. "That's right. They are."

She shook her head, feeling totally confused. "I don't understand. Shouldn't you be sending them to Sara then?"

Sadness now etched lines on Tyler's face. "Oh, I'm sorry, I forgot that you don't know about her. You see, Sara was Rosalind's daughter. She died four years ago."

Chapter Three

Zelda sensed that she had stumbled onto a sensitive subject, and one on which she felt certain Tyler would not care to elaborate. The nature of Tyler's relationship with Rosalind and Sara, or with any of the Redmonds for that matter, was totally his own business. She stirred uneasily in her chair, looking down at her hands to keep from looking at Tyler. "I'll make sure to get you Rosalind's address first thing in the morning."

Just as Zelda was saying this, their waitress arrived with their dessert. "My, this looks delicious. What do you call it?" Zelda asked quickly, relieved to find a new subject to talk about.

"It's a Sicilian pastry horn, and the filling is Ricotta cheese with chopped mixed candied peel and pistachio nuts, and it's his favorite dessert," she said, nodding her head toward Tyler. "It's really popular with everyone. I hope you enjoy it."

"I'm sure I will. Everything I've eaten here is marvelous." Zelda said enthusiastically.

"You're one of the preferred customers around here, I think," Zelda told Tyler as soon as the pretty, olive-skinned girl walked away from their table. "You rate special attention, that's for sure. That cute little Italian girl even knows your favorite dessert."

"I told you I eat here often. And it helps that I'm a really good friend of the owner's son, Joe Vinelli." He smiled with appealing candor.

Zelda's eyes widened with interest. "Joe Vinelli, the jockey, you mean?"

"That's the guy."

"I've watched him on the Keeneland Race Course countless times. I've seen him on television too in the Kentucky Derby, the Preakness, and Belmont. He's getting up there in the winner's class right along with Pat Day, Gary Stevens, Chris McCarron, and my dad's favorite jockey, Jerry Bailey."

"Joe's got what it takes all right. Besides that, he's a thoroughly nice fellow, and a devoted friend. Would you like to meet him sometime?" Tyler asked, cocking his head toward her.

"Sure, I'd love to. In fact I think it's high time that someone like me who was born and raised in the 'Horse Capital of the World' where champion thoroughbreds are bred, foaled, trained, bought, sold, raced, and retired gets to meet a famous jockey face to face when he doesn't have a horse under him," she answered, her eyes bright with merriment.

"You're about five-foot-three. I expect you and Joe could stand and talk eyeball to eyeball. He gave her an amused grin. "Joe's like Napoleon, not too tall but plenty heroic."

"And very good looking too."

"Hold on now! I'm not introducing you to my competition," he said wryly. "I had trouble enough to get you away from business long enough to have dinner with me."

She contemplated him, a benign smile on her face. "You've nothing to fear, Tyler. Who could possibly be more captivating than a man who's all heart?"

His eyes touched hers and for the briefest moment, amusement seemed to glimmer between them. "I know you're razzing me, but I consider that an encouraging sign."

"Oh, you do?"

"Yes, I do. And if you'll get busy and finish your dessert, I could be persuaded to take you to a movie."

"Oh, you think you could?" There was a pleasant curve to Zelda's mouth.

"Yeah, I think it's pretty likely."

Zelda's eyes now glinted with good-humored mischief, and she quickly picked up her fork and took a large bite of the pastry horn.

As soon as Zelda got to work the following morning, she called Barton Redmond at the bank. She was told that Barton hadn't come in yet that morning, so she asked if she might speak with Mathew Redmond.

"May I tell him who's calling?" the reception- ist asked in a carefully modulated, elegant sounding voice intended to convey to the caller that he or she was speaking to an important, fi- nancial institution.

"Zelda Iverson of Iverson Sales," Zelda an- swered in a pleasant, business like tone.

Almost immediately Mathew was on the line. "Zelda, it's nice to hear from you."

"I need a bit of information for our records and I wasn't able to reach your father. I wonder if you could give me your aunt Rosalind Trask's address."

"Sure thing, just hold on a second while I flip through my Rolodex. Yeah—here it is. That's Mrs. Edward Trask—and I'll give you Ed's busi- ness address because Rosalind and Ed live part of the year in Portugal. The Trask Seafood Company has canneries in Lisbon as well as Seattle, and the company's address is the best way to keep up with them."

Zelda jotted down the address Mathew gave her, and then before he might question her about why she would need to contact Rosalind, she quickly said, "I know you're busy so I won't keep you. But I do thank you for your help."

"Hey, don't hang up. I'm not all that busy, and besides I wanted to ask you something." There was an urgent note in his usually polished voice. "Was that you I saw last night coming out of Villa Vinelli with Ty Wakefield?"

"It could have been. We did have dinner there."

"Well, I was surprised. I had no idea you two were old friends," he said with quiet emphasis.

"We're actually new friends," she answered indulgently, aware that he was sounding her out. "We met at your estate sale, as a matter of fact. I believe I told your father that Tyler came by on the day of the pre-sale. Of course, I couldn't allow him to go in because his name was not on the invited list. It was an odd situation. I figured your dad would have mentioned it to you since your grandfather evidently had known Tyler for some time."

"He may have. I just don't remember," he said

grudgingly. "Besides, I have something more interesting to talk about, and I'd like to ask a favor
of you."

"Sure, what is it?"

"Well, it's like this." He hesitated for a second
and cleared his throat. "You see, the wife of one
of the directors on the board of our bank is the
chairman for the Charity League Horse Show
this year. The big fund-raising dinner is a week
from Saturday, and since I'm representing our
bank as a sponsor, Gloria Sandefur and her husband have asked me to sit at the head table with
them. It's sort of a command performance, you
understand." He chuckled with a dry and cynical
sound. "And by all means I need a charming and
beautiful date. That would be you, Zelda." He
said in his smooth, deep voice.

Zelda was stunned by the totally unexpected
idea of Mathew Redmond asking her for a date
of any sort, and his wanting her to accompany
him to a large social affair like this one made no
sense to her at all. Certainly he hadn't planned
on asking her before this very moment. He
scarcely knew her. The business of the estate sale
had brought them together. There was nothing
social in their brief acquaintance.

"I—I don't know what to say, Mathew. That's
very nice of you—and I'm flattered that you
thought of me—but." She kept stammering as

she struggled for just what to say. "I—well, I mean for a special occasion like this, I'm sure there's someone in your group of friends who would know most of the people there and has been anxiously waiting for you to invite her to go with you. As for me, I wouldn't know anyone and I'd only recognize a few faces of some people who frequent our estate and consignment sales."

"All the more reason you must come with me. I've a lot a people I'd like to introduce you to. They could be potential clients. So that would be good for Iverson's business. Who knows, you might find out that you enjoy my company."

"I'm sure I would," she said, trying to sound as gracious as she could.

"Then I take it we have a date for a week from Saturday."

"Looks like we do," she agreed with an uneasy laugh. There was a bemused look on Zelda's face as she hung up the phone. There was something very odd about this. It made her uncomfortable because she had a strong feeling that there was an ulterior motive behind this interest Mathew had suddenly taken in her.

Not wanting to take time to speculate about that now, she grabbed the phone again and called Tyler. "I've got Rosalind's address for you," she told him, explaining why he needed to use the

Trask company address in Seattle and that they'd forward it to Lisbon if she were there.

"Was Barton surprised that you wanted to know how to reach his sister?" Tyler asked curiously.

"Barton wasn't at the bank when I called. I talked to Mathew."

"Well I bet he quizzed you thoroughly."

"No, not about that. He thought it was for our records because of the estate sale. He didn't question it at all."

"Good. Glad he didn't give you any static. And thanks for helping me out."

"No problem," she hesitated, wanting to say more about Mathew, but not sure whether she should or not." "But, you know, Mathew did question me about knowing you," she said, decisively, telling herself nothing ventured nothing gained.

"Hmm—I wonder what made him think we were acquainted?"

"He said he saw me with you at Villa Vinelli's last night."

"I sure didn't see him in there, did you?" Tyler's voice rose inquiringly.

"Oh he wasn't inside the restaurant. He said he saw us as we were leaving."

"He may have seen us, but I sure didn't see him. Frankly, I'm surprised he was around there.

He doesn't usually frequent the same sort of places I do." His words held just the slightest tinge of contempt.

"I guess he was just making conversation, but he did wonder if we were old friends."

Tyler snickered. "Sure, of course he did. What did you tell him?"

"The truth. That we'd met at the estate sale."

"What did he say to that?"

"Nothing—just started talking about something else."

"That's just as well. I can't see Mathew giving me any great build-up." Tyler gave a wry chuckle. "He figures he's got dibs on every beautiful girl in Lexington. He's just put out because I saw you first."

"Is this your way of saying that you think I'm pretty?—in a businesslike way, of course," she asked playfully.

"In every kind of way, Zelda; and not just pretty—I said beautiful."

His voice, deep and sensual, sent a shiver through her. They were flirting with each other, more or less, and she realized she was by no means blind to his attraction. "Flattery will get you everything," she said facetiously.

"Is that a promise or a threat?" Tyler countered glibly.

She laughed. "A little bit of both maybe."

"Well then, the first thing I'd like to get is for you to come out to my place on Sunday afternoon and see my new colt. I want you to pick out exactly the right name for him."

"You can't be serious. You wouldn't let me name your prize thoroughbred horse."

"Sure I would. Why not?"

"Because I've heard breeders have strong feelings about the names they choose for their thoroughbred horses. They're even superstitious about it, because it has to be a lucky name, one that sounds like a winner. Isn't that right?"

"Whether it is or not, come Sunday you're going to give my new colt a name. And I'm a superstitious breeder who believes that will be lucky for all of us."

Zelda was smiling as she hung up the phone. Everything about this conversation with Tyler made her feel good. She left the office and walked with buoyant steps into the gallery show room where she was going to get everything in order for the upcoming consignment sale. She hummed and sang snatches of pop songs as she worked.

Chapter Four

There are 450 horse farms in and around Lexington and they represent both a deep-seated tradition and a thriving modern industry. Zelda had toured one or two in the past, but she had a special and more personal interest in this first visit to Tyler's farm.

There's nothing quite like driving the back roads surrounding Lexington where sites border on the dramatic: grazing and galloping horses, lush meadows and extravagant barns, miles of pristine white or historic limestone fences. These hand-laid stone fences stand testament to the people of Kentucky's special relationship with the land. For in the ancient limestone that rests just below the land's surface lies the core to everything that is the Bluegrass—lush rolling fields, and the world's fastest horses.

Tyler had told her that it was about a twenty-five minute drive to his farm, and when she got there she'd follow along about a quarter mile of white fencing before she'd catch sight of his house. At this particular moment she was following alongside one of the old limestone rock fences on a pleasant country road shaded by a canopy of trees. At the next crossroad, she turned off to the right and almost immediately caught sight of neat white fences stretching out ahead of her, enclosing what seemed like miles of green pastures. In a few minutes, however, she saw the long wooden stables and outbuildings painted white with bright green trim and matching green roofs.

A short distance beyond, a long drive shadowed by tall, ancient trees led to a one-and-a-half story farm house. A deep wood porch with square columns set on stone piers extended across the front and Greek Revival pilasters and cornice moldings complemented the house's white painted clapboard siding.

Apparently Tyler had been waiting for her, because as she drew near the house he came striding off the porch to greet her as she got out of her car. "You didn't have any problems finding my place did you." He made it more a statement than a question.

"None at all. I knew just how to come. Fact is I was out in this exact area recently to gather up some items for a consignment sale. You know that plantation house in the valley just about two miles before you come to where you turn onto your road. A couple named Martin own it."

"You're talking about the place they call MARTINDALE."

"Yeah, that's it. Do you know Phillip and Linda Martin?"

"In sort of a round about way I do."

She glanced at him curiously. "Round-a-bout—how do you know somebody round and about? Is that anything like knowing them up and down, or forward and backward," she teased with a ripple of laughter.

Tyler grimaced in good humor. "You successful business women are so literal. What I should have said is that the contractor who did a modest amount of remodeling on my place did a major amount of work on the Martin's antebellum home. Through our mutual contractor I became briefly acquainted with the Martins."

"Oooh, I find that most interesting. Tell me, did you find a treasure hidden in your stairwell like the Martins did?"

"A what—in my where?" He eyed her as if he thought she had lost her mind.

"They unearthed a Confederate sword, and some antique silver under the stairs in the Martin's house during their remodeling. I just wondered if you discovered something valuable beneath your staircase too."

He shook his head. "Nothing like that in my house, I'm afraid. First place, the Martins have a finer, larger home that was built much earlier than this 1930's farmhouse of mine. The only things found here were a dozen or so Mason jars for canning and about twenty-five years worth of old *National Geographic* magazines."

"Well, you wouldn't have had much use for a Confederate sword anyway," she said with a smile that turned into a chuckle. "So now tell me all about your Wakefield Farm and show me around your place." She held out her hand to him as as she said this. "I want to see everything."

"Come on then." He grabbed her hand. "I'll give you the grand tour."

"Good! And I hope you'll provide interesting commentary as we go along. I'm really interested to hear the who, why, what, when, where and how."

Tyler laughed. "That's practically my life story, Zelda. You think you have time to hear all that? Remember you do have to save enough time to name this new colt for me."

"It's only two o'clock in the afternoon Tyler. How long do you think it will take?"

"As long as I can persuade you to stay," he quipped, giving her a teasing glance and tightening his hold on her hand.

She arched her brows, eyeing him coyly. "Then I best warn you, Tyler, that on a Sunday afternoon date I always go home before dark."

"Well then, it's certainly a good thing that I ordered the pizzas to be delivered at six o'clock." There was humor in his eyes and a sly curve to his mouth.

Puzzled, Zelda frowned at him. "What are you talking about?"

"Our supper, of course. Surely you didn't think I'd get you out here and hike you all around my eighty acre horse farm, and then not feed you before I let you go home."

"I think you're putting me on Tyler. In the first place, I doubt that there's any place in Lexington that would deliver this far out. And even if they would, their hefty delivery charge would exceed the price of the pizzas."

Tyler lifted one shoulder in an off-hand shrug. "You're wrong. No charge to a guy with my connections."

"Oh sure," she countered, showing her disbelief in the tone of her voice. "You just have to tip him a bundle."

"No way," Tyler shook his head. "My man doesn't accept a tip. He's just going to stay and eat with us."

Nonplussed, she stared at him, trying to figure out what he was up to. "Are you playing some sort of joke on me, Tyler?"

"Maybe just a little. You said you wanted to meet a jockey. So the fellow who's bringing us our pizzas is Joe Vinelli."

"Really, *the* Joe Vinelli?" she asked, not at all certain she could believe him.

"In the flesh, I kid you not."

Zelda smiled. "Looks like this is turning into a day of new experiences for me. I get to name a thoroughbred, eat pizza with a celebrated jockey, and learn the story behind this horse farm of yours, all in the same afternoon. Can't get any better than that."

"Let's have at it then," Tyler said. And as he slipped an arm around her waist urging her forward, his chuckle was rich and intimate.

Zelda enjoyed the easy camaraderie they were sharing. It caused an unexpected ripple of contentment to rush through her. "All right, tell me how you got started in this business of raising thoroughbreds."

"Well, like I said. It's pretty much the story

of my life. My parents both worked, and I didn't have any brothers or sisters to hang around with. But I did have a buddy, Brian Kent was his name, and we were best friends from third grade through high school. After school and all day Saturday we were together at Green Glen Farm. You may know it. It's not far from Keeneland race course."

"I know where you mean. There are a number of farms out that way that were on one of the visitor tours. Dad and I took my aunt when she came from Colorado one summer."

"Brian's dad was the manager at Green Glen and the two of us hung out there. We did chores for his dad, and when we got old enough and had a little training we were allowed to groom and exercise some of the horses. Then it wasn't long after that that we really became a bonafide part of the working staff of Green Glen. Brian and I worked all day Saturday and after school on weekdays, during the school term and full time in the summers. It was a neat time for Brian and me, and we were getting paid for it to boot. We thought that was plenty cool." Though he said this lightly, and with a sort of off hand shrug, Zelda sensed that this had been a time of singular importance in Tyler's life.

"Sounds plenty cool to me," Zelda said, studying him, a gleam of interest in her eyes. "So what happened after you graduated from high school?"

"Oh man, that summer was the best yet."

"How's that?"

"Well first it was that summer that Nathan Redmond bought Sweet Dream for Sara. He reappeared to have her horse boarded at Green Glen, and engaged me to work with Sara and Sweet Dream in what is called hippo-therapy."

"For heaven sake, what is that? I never heard of it." She looked mystified.

"The funny part is that at the time I didn't know anything about it either. But believe me, Nathan saw to it that I got familiar with the program of therapy in very short order."

Zelda frowned. "I still haven't the slightest notion of what this hippo whatever is, and even less about how Sara and her horse fit in with it."

Tyler smiled. "I know you like to know all the what, why, where and all. Just give me a chance to explain." He teased her good naturedly. "You know about antiques and all that ancient Greek and Roman stuff. So you probably know that hippo is Greek for horse. Thus hippo-therapy is simply using a horse as physical therapist for adults and kids with polio, cerebral palsy, muscular dystrophy and other disabilities."

"Oh I hope nothing that serious was wrong with Sara."

"Well, the way Nathan explained it was that due to a birth injury, she was affected with cerebral palsy. But that term covers a wide range of disabilities that are not unsurmountable. With Sara it was muscle weakness, and problems with balance and coordination. Nathan and Sara were convinced that with daily therapy with Sweet Dream she could overcome all obstacles and be a normal, active teenager just like every other girl about to enter high school."

"And did that happen, Tyler?"

"Gradually—but it took more than that first summer for Sara to realize her dream, I'm afraid." His tone had a note of warmth and concern. Therapeutic riding isn't all that easy. There are a lot of procedures you have to follow."

"Tell me about how it worked with Sara and you?"

"Well, basically riding stimulates the muscles, so riding bareback is the standard approach. That way it let Sara feel the horse's muscles as it walked, causing Sara's body to respond with a rhythmic shift from side to side. And as with any exercise, her muscles grew stronger every week. Of course, in those early sessions that first summer, Sara mainly had to focus on relaxing and feeling comfortable on Sweet Dream's back. She had to twist and turn, reach up high and down to her toes, then reach forward to Sweet Dream's head and backward to her tail, all to improve her balance and coordination."

"Sounds like quite a workout, and I imagine it was far from easy for Sara." Zelda gave a sympathetic sigh. "She must have been quite an exceptional girl."

"She was that," Tyler agreed. "And a totally determined one to boot," he added, a slight tremor of emotion in his voice. "I can't tell you how many times I had to keep reminding her to breathe, because when she would concentrate so hard on the range-of-motion exercises, she'd forget the basic need of breathing." He paused for a few seconds, looking off toward the barn that they were coming up to. "I don't think I'll ever forget that day when Sara first rode on the training track for Nathan to see. She was relaxed and holding the reins with confidence. And she rode around the ring, swaying her hips right to left in sync with Sweet Dream's gait. Nathan was so excited. He handed me his camera. 'You get busy taking pictures,' he ordered. 'This is the most significant happening in Sara's life so far.' I never saw Nathan that emotional before."

"Were some of the pictures you took that day among the ones you found in that cardboard box?" Zelda asked. For she was now more curious than ever about this granddaughter of Nathan Redmond's. From what Tyler had just told her, it was quite apparent that he had played a very important part in Sara's life. Most likely it would follow that this young, vulnerable girl had a major role in Tyler's life too.

"Sure! Most likely all of them. I'm sure Nathan kept every snapshot there ever was of Sara."

"Well I hope you haven't mailed them all off to Rosalind already. I'd like to see them."

"Oh, too bad. I sent them out the same day you gave me the address. However, I've got some pictures of her at the house you can see later. Right now you're going to see Sweet Dream and have a look at the colt you're going to name for me," Tyler said, swinging wide the door into the barn.

There was so much more that Zelda wanted to hear about. He still hadn't told her how and when he acquired his farm. She recalled that first day when they'd met that Tyler called Nathan his benefactor. Perhaps that was a clue. It suddenly struck her that Nathan would have wanted to do a lot for the young man who had succeeded in improving the quality of Sara's life. But Zelda wasn't going to learn about this now, for they were inside the barn and Tyler was intent on showing her his horses.

"We have two of these twelve-stall barns, each with a run out into a paddock so the mares can go back and forth. The second barn and paddock is several hundred yards south of this one. Then a good ways over to the east is the breeding shed and the stables where I have our two quality stakes winner stallions. You probably noticed those out buildings as you drove up."

She nodded. "I saw a lot of white structures with green roofs surrounded by white fencing. So I guess I did." She widened her eyes, breathing a surprised exclamation through her circled lips. "You know, you've got quite a place here. Three barns and all those stalls and paddocks—you must own twenty–five or more thoroughbreds."

"Whoa there," Tyler halted her, holding up a discounting hand. "Don't get any wrong ideas here. Not all these mares are mine. You see I board horses, and a number of brood mares are brought to me to be bred with my stallion. As a matter of fact when I started out seven years ago, Wakefield Farm had only six mares including Sweet Dream. I now have twelve. Also I bought my second stallion, Bold and Bronze, just a little over a year ago. He's the sire of Sweet Dream's foal, which means that this colt could have tremendous potential." He put his arm around her waist and squeezed her affectionately. "So let's stop talking and go down to that last stall on the right and let you see and name this future star-quality champion. Who, if I'm really lucky, could make a dream of mine come true." Tyler spoke the words lightly, but an eager look shone in his eyes.

Chapter Five

"He's incredible!" Zelda exclaimed, gazing at the balance and symmetry of the colt standing close beside the brood mare Tyler had talked about so often. The young horse's glossy chestnut coat was slightly darker and more red than the sorrel-brown colored Sweet Dream. "He's so handsome, and I'm guessing that he got his elegant bronze-colored coat from his sire Bold and Bronze. Am I right?"

Tyler nodded. "Right as rain."

"But that pretty blaze of white on his face matches Sweet Dream's. I love horses with that sort of mark. They look so classy and elegant to me."

"Yeah, his face is like Sweet Dream's all right,

and I'm glad of that. He's got the distinguishing features of both his dam and sire. Did you notice his different colored feet?" Tyler led Zelda into the stall. "See, he's got two white feet and two black feet, just like ol' Bold and Bronze."

Zelda eyed the colt in amazement. "Isn't that unusual?" she queried, sounding surprised.

"No, not at all. Of course lots of horses have all four feet that match, but just as many will have one or two feet white and the rest dark like Sweet Dream. I've even seen several with three white and only one dark. What do you think of that?" he asked, angling his head at her.

Zelda wrinkled her nose at him and shrugged. "I think I'm not very observant when it comes to the lower half of a horse. Probably because I'm usually looking at them in a race and their legs move so fast it's all sort of a blur."

Tyler laughed. "Well, I'll take you to your next race and we'll check out each thoroughbred as he walks down the track to the starting gate. I think I can point out several interesting things about race horses that you might not have noticed before."

It was her turn to angle her head at him. "I'll bet you can at that," she said, as her smiling eyes met his. "I've had a preliminary lesson today."

"Yeah, I guess once I get to talking about this

new colt of mine there's no shutting me up," he said with a self-deprecating shrug.

"Oh that's fine. I want to hear everything you can tell me. You see, I need to know all these things about him in order to give him a proper name. One that truly fits him."

He narrowed, his eyes at her questioningly. "Well, Zelda, just don't think that because of this conversation about his feet that you're going to name him something weird like White Socks," Tyler said, a teasing glint of humor now in his eyes.

"Heavens no—Never!" She wrinkled her nose in distaste. "I'm going to pick a name for him that's perfect. I want it to sound pretty when you say it, and it has to be symbolic too." There was fervor in her voice and she raised her hand in a fist and shook it at him emphatically.

"You bet it does," he agreed wholeheartedly. "Right now, though, it's time for these two to get out of this barn and into the fresh air and sunshine." As he stated this, he led the mare and her colt out of the stall and Zelda watched as they trotted out into the paddock. "Come on," he said turning to Zelda and grabbing her hand in his firm grasp. "I need to show you the rest of my place."

The afternoon sunlight was clear and bright as brass after the shadowy interior of the barn.

Overhead, the April sky was a hyacinth blue with a spray of feathery clouds fanning out across space. They ambled leisurely along and Tyler pointed out the outbuildings that he'd mentioned earlier. They were circling back going in the direction of Tyler's house when Zelda caught sight of another building. It too was white, but it had numerous windows flanked with green shutters. "What's that?" she asked, pointing toward it. "It sure doesn't look like your other barns. It looks more like a house."

"That's because it is a house," he said, laughing. "That's where Ernie and his wife live."

"Who's Ernie?"

"He's my assistant and right-hand man. In fact, without Nathan's backing and Ernie's experience and hard work to help me make a go of it, there would be no Wakefield Farm." There was a faint tremor of emotion in his voice.

"That's why you said Nathan was your benefactor, isn't it?"

"That's one of the reasons, Zelda. Nathan Redmond was a man who cared about people and his compassion knew no bounds. He made a lot of things possible for me." There was a contemplative expression on his face as he said this, and his low voice seemed to come from a long way off.

"I'd like to know how Wakefield Farm started,

if you wouldn't mind telling me that is," she said softly.

"No, I don't mind, but are you sure you want to hear the rest of the Tyler Wakefield story."

"Absolutely certain," Zelda declared.

Tyler's face creased into an arresting smile. "Okay then, tell me where I left off earlier."

"You were telling me about that first summer you started working with Sara and Sweet Dream—the horse therapy thing."

"Yeah," he bobbed his head in agreement. "That was sort of the first milestone in my relationship with Nathan." He paused, rubbing his hand across the curve of his chin reflectively. After a second he continued. "I started college that next fall, and since the university is here in Lexington I was able to continue working part time at Green Glen. And of course, I worked every summer. So, four years after I graduated, I became business manager at Green Glen with a very respectable salary. I did all the accounting and bookkeeping, kept inventory of supplies, handled orders, and did the monthly billing on the horses that were being boarded at Green Glen or brought there to be bred. Then I began to grasp the whole nine yards of this business, and I started planning and dreaming of how I could save enough money by the time I was thirty to have my very own horse farm." He said the words with the certainty of a man who could never be satisfied with only a dream.

"Oh Tyler, you're giving me goose bumps." She shivered with excitement, rubbing her arms vigorously. "Here you have this wonderful place of your own, everything you wanted, why you've had it for what three or four years?—and you're probably not even thirty yet."

"Hold on now. That's not totally accurate." He grimaced in good humor. "Actually, I've had this farm for a little over six years, and I'm going on thirty two."

"You owned your own horse farm at the age of twenty-five, Tyler, that's quite an accomplishment," she said, a look of admiration in her eyes and praise in her voice.

He shrugged. "Well the bank and I owned it is more like it," he said candidly. "But when this place suddenly came up for sale, Nathan convinced me that I'd never have such an excellent opportunity again and I must grab it up. You see Nathan's bank held a mortgage on it. So Nathan had all the inside information and realized a really good deal might be made, because the owner had just died and his only heir was a nephew in California, who was a script writer for a television comedy series and had not the slightest interest in a horse farm in Kentucky. All he wanted to do was sell it as fast as he could. Nathan believed that he'd accept any half-way reasonable offer just to get it off his hands."

"And obviously he did—accept a half-way reasonable offer, that is," she mocked him, a warm smile curving her lips.

He laughed. "We made a fair deal that satisfied both of us."

"And presto, just like that you owned an eighty-acre horse farm," Zelda said gaily.

"After Nathan arranged for me to get the loan I needed, I did. But let me tell you, I spent a lot of time pinching myself to prove it was all real."

They had been walking slowly ahead as they talked. Now as they came close to the house with the green shutters, Zelda gave a little exclamation of delight. Yellow jonquils, like sunshine, shared a garden of narcissus and paperwhites at the front of the house. Purple striped crocus were scattered here and there in the grass of the front lawn, and there were roses greening on an arbor nearby. "Your right-hand man, Ernie, is something of a gardener, judging from all these pretty flowers," she exclaimed, pausing to admire everything.

"Not really," Tyler said, shaking his head. "Ernie doesn't shun mowing, or digging—nothing like that. But it's his wife, Martha who's responsible for everything that blooms around here. She like things pretty and colorful. Wait until you see all that she planted at my house," he cocked an eyebrow wryly, "and hear the reasons she gave for doing it."

She narrowed her eyes at him. "What? I'm curious. Tell me about it."

"Well first you need to know that Ernie and Martha's son is in the nursery business in Louisville. Whenever he gets overstocked or wants to clear out some plants and shrubs, he trucks the stuff down to his mother. Consequently, a couple of years ago he brought her sixty or more azaleas, most of which were either coral red or white. Martha had room for only about ten at her house, so she made Ernie and me prepare beds around my house and she planted all the rest of them there. She claimed that my house lacked color, and a woman's touch, and what I needed to do was find myself a wife who loved flowers and horses and me."

"Did she mean in that order?" Zelda asked, laughing.

Tyler shrugged. "I guess so. I didn't dare ask. Martha is very positive about things. One doesn't question her about her suggestions."

"So what did you tell her?" Zelda asked.

Tyler looked at her with a glint of amusement in his eyes. "I intimated that I'd get started looking—take advantage of any opportunity that presented itself." He answered glibly.

"And I bet you've had numerous opportunities," she countered, prodding him playfully.

"Some, of course." Tyler lifted one shoulder in an off-hand shrug that Zelda found charming. "But not any great number. You see, I don't get out to all that many interesting places, and the last time I did, I got turned away at the door."

"Oh, Tyler," she protested. "You know I couldn't help it. Are you always going to hold that against me?"

"No," he said quickly, his arms encircling her waist. "I'd much rather hold you against me."

Suddenly beneath their light banter, Zelda felt a note of romance. "That was a sneaky little maneuver of yours," she said, in a voice that was smoky soft.

"Yeah—well a guy just has to take advantage of any opportunity, you know." He smiled down at her, and the allure in his eyes took her breath away. "Worked out rather nicely, though, don't you think?"

His face was only inches from hers, and she felt the warmth of his breath on her face. He brushed a light, gentle kiss across her forehead. Then he wrapped his arms more securely around her, bent his head and his lips slowly descended to meet hers. Zelda enjoyed the sweet tenderness of his kiss, for though it was brief, she experienced an intimacy in it that surprised her and did unruly things to her heart.

Tyler let her ease away from his embrace, but he kept one arm around her waist as they started walking the remaining distance back to Tyler's house. Zelda slipped her arm around his waist and lengthened her step as Tyler shortened his. Now they walked side by side in perfect unison. A smile of contentment wreathed Zelda's face, because at that moment it occurred to her that she would enjoy walking most anywhere with this man at her side.

Joe Vinelli arrived right on time at six o'clock, bringing with him two melt-in-your-mouth pizzas fresh from Vinelli's restaurant. "The cheese on these still looks hot and bubbly," Zelda said, opening the box lids and smelling the delicious aroma of the two varieties of toppings.

"Yeah, Joe here, believes in covering ground at break-neck speed whether he's got a car or a horse under him." Tyler ribbed his friend, good naturedly.

"Well, you don't win a race if your horse is the last one out of the gate, now do you?" Joe stated, with an engaging twinkle in his eyes.

Zelda didn't know what she expected jockeys to be like, but Joe Vinelli was more than she ever could have imagined. He was full of antics and jokes, having a sense of humor that never quit.

He had a small build, as jockeys do, and was so well coordinated that his agile movements were like those of a trained dancer. Perhaps the thing Zelda found so appealing in Joe's personality was that there was even a touch of whimsy about him like an erstwhile Peter Pan.

The three of them sat around an oak pedestal table in Tyler's kitchen eating wedges of pizza, the fellows drinking cola while Zelda had iced tea. Zelda plied Joe with questions about his recent races, and asked where he might be racing between now and the Kentucky Derby in May.

"I'm going to race at Santa Anita in April, but about the Derby it's still a little early to know," he told her. "But I'll tell you this, two years from now I'm counting on riding Tyler's new horse in his first stakes ride."

"If he's good enough, you'll sure be the one to ride him," Tyler agreed. "We're all just doing a lot of wishful thinking at this early stage of the game. Lots of work and a good trainer have to get into the act first."

Joe turned his attention to Zelda. "And speaking of Ty's high hopes colt, I understand he's given you the honor of naming him."

She nodded. "I'm surprised he's letting me pick his name, but I'm sure going to make it a good one."

"Well just let me say this much. Maybe this

colt is going to make it for Tyler—maybe not. But you give him a name to live up to." He smiled and pushed back from the table. "With that little bit of pep talk, I'm going to high tail it out of here, 'cause I've got a plane to catch first thing in the morning for California." With this Joe left as fast as he'd come.

Several minutes later, Zelda told Tyler she must be going too. "It's been a super afternoon. I've enjoyed every minute," she said, as they walked out of the kitchen.

"Good. Just hope my show and tell of Wake-field Farm didn't wear you out too much."

"No way," she said, shaking her head and smiling. "I learned some very interesting things, and I want to tell you I really like your horses."

"As much as you like flowers?" he asked, amusement flickering in his eyes as they met hers.

"Oh, even more than flowers," she retorted, bringing her hand up to her lips to supress her laughter.

"I'll report that to Martha." Tyler grinned as he said this, and then warm, rich laughter floated up from his throat. It was an infectious sound and Zelda laughed too.

They reached the front door and Zelda held a finger to her lips to shush him. "Get serious now, Tyler. Before I go I want to tell you that I have a name for Sweet Dream's colt."

Instantly Tyler grew serious, his eyes widening with interest. "I'm all ears. What is it?"

Suddenly Zelda felt shy with him. "Look—if you—I mean if you don't like it," she stammered, "well, it's okay. You don't need to take it. I mean, I want it to be right, and we can come up with another name that you do like."

"Zelda—stop hedging for goodness sake. Just tell me. What is it?"

She ran her tongue over lips nervously. "Well, it's Dream Maker."

"Dream Maker! That's it!" Tyler's voice boomed like loud speakers at a rock concert. "Dream Maker—it's positively the perfect name for him. It couldn't be anything else." Tyler's voice echoed the elation sparkling in his eyes. He reached out and cupped her face between his warm hands. His eyes held hers and something stretched between them, a feeling that Tyler put into words. "This horse is going to live up to the name you've given him Zelda. He'll be a dream maker, you just wait and see."

Chapter Six

Zelda was a little uneasy about what she should wear to the Charity League dinner with Mathew. Especially since they were to be sitting at the head table. It was a black-tie affair, so that called for her to wear something dressy. Somehow she doubted that she had anything in her present wardrobe that provided the chic elegance that this occasion called for.

On the first of the week, she explained her predicament to her father. He, good naturedly, gave her the day off to go shopping. During the earlier part of the day she went to the stores where she usually shopped, but she found nothing that was more suitable than outfits she already had. Mid-afternoon, she decided to try a specialty shop that she only frequented when they were having sales. She tried on several things that fit well and looked nice on her. All were quite lovely, in fact, but one was totally irresistible. It was a three piece cocktail suit in beautiful imported silk fabric. The pencil slim skirt and hip-length jacket were in a rich, peacock blue. The jewel neck blouse was the softest shade of shell pink and the neckline and the edges of the cap sleeves were banded with two rows of tiny iridescent beads.

Zelda turned around slowly looking at herself from every angle. Yes, this suit was perfect for her in every detail, and she felt exactly right in it. She took a deep breath before looking at the price tag, crossing her fingers that the price wouldn't be outrageous. It was costly but not prohibitive. She exhaled and smiled at her reflection in the dressing room mirror.

Zelda hadn't expected it, but there was a stir of interest as she and Mathew leisurely moved through the large dining area on their way to the head table. Many people, most of them women, spoke to Mathew. He greeted them all warmly and introduced Zelda, stopping to chat for a few minutes before moving on.

In her new outfit, Zelda was confident that she looked her best. Mathew was extraordinarily handsome, and he was looking remarkably lean, broad shouldered, and impeccable in his tuxedo. Zelda sensed that he was well aware of this fact and enjoying every admiring glance he was getting. She could see that Mathew was a man for women. It was obvious that women of all ages were drawn to him. Zelda would admit that Mathew had considerable charm, yet somehow he didn't really appeal to her that much.

Though in the beginning she hadn't been too eager to attend this affair with Mathew, as the evening progressed, she had to confess that she was having a most enjoyable time. However, she still couldn't figure out why Mathew had asked her.

"You know you made a big hit with Gloria and George Sandefur tonight," Mathew told her as he drove her home after the dinner. "So much so, in fact, that she made me promise to bring you to the party at their home, following the horse show. Of course, I said we'd be there. That's all right with you, isn't it." He smiled at her, totally confident of her affirmative answer.

Zelda gave a non-committal shrug. "My goodness, the Charity League Horse Show is a couple of months away—sometime in July, isn't it?"

"Yeah, it was mid-July last year. In the meantime, I'd like to take you to a fun place this coming Friday night—where we can eat and talk and get better acquainted."

Zelda shook her head. "I'm afraid I'll be busy working next weekend. We're having our big spring consignment sale at Iverson's."

"Well, what do you say we do something in the middle of the week?—say Tuesday or Wednesday?"

"Really, I can't do anything during the week. I'm a working girl you know. In our business we're setting up for a sale, having the sale, or inventorying and making all the necessary preparations for an estate sale. To be honest I have very little time for socializing, I'm afraid." She gave him a benign smile.

Mathew eyed her skeptically. "You're seeing someone else. That's it, isn't it?"

He was giving her an out, so Zelda grabbed on to it. "Well yes, I do see someone a little."

"Someone like Ty Wakefield—no doubt." Mathew's jaw tensed in irritation.

Zelda didn't know what to say to this. She didn't want to discuss Tyler with Mathew and she didn't intend to. "Look, let's not spoil things. You asked me to help you out tonight and it has been a special evening. One that I've enjoyed very much," she said, in a soft, cajoling voice. "On a regular basis, though, the right girl for you is one who's free to go places with you as often as you want. I'm simply not that girl."

Mathew's tight lipped expression mirrored his irritation. "Okay, I'll accept that for now," he said, tersely. "Only let me tell you this. Ty Wakefield is not the right guy for you. Sure, he may have been the fair haired boy for Nathan and Rosalind, and everybody knows how Sara loved him, but you'd be smart to give me a chance. You see, Zelda, I don't have all the emotional baggage hanging on me that Ty does. You think about that!" With these cryptic words, Mathew walked her to her door, then with a brief "good night," he left.

Zelda didn't know what to make of Mathew's peevish behavior nor the odd statement he'd made concerning Tyler. *Emotional baggage*— what exactly did Mathew mean to imply when he said Tyler had emotional baggage hanging on him? Was he referring to Nathan, Rosalind or Sara—possibly all three of them—or even none of them? She frowned, feeling both confused and annoyed. She knew Mathew was disgruntled because she had not been eager to spend time with him. He wasn't accustomed to being turned down when he asked for a date. She probably was the only one who'd ever said no to him, she thought wryly. Actually, though, she didn't think it mattered so much to Mathew that she'd sort of brushed him off, as it did that she was willing to go out with Tyler. That was the thing that bothered him the most.

She heaved a weary sigh and headed for her bedroom. There were bad feelings of some kind between Mathew and Tyler. She'd sensed this all along. That was their problem, however, not hers. And as for carrying around emotional baggage, everybody does at least a little of that. She shouldn't let what Mathew said about Tyler concern her. Still, she couldn't help being curious as to what sort of emotional baggage it was. And just how great an affect was it having on Tyler's life?

Iverson's big spring consignment sale was set for the following weekend, so Zelda spent more time than usual at the store in preparation for it. She was just getting ready to leave on Thursday, just before six, when the phone rang and it was Tyler. Since this was the first time she'd talked to him this week, their conversation started off with some pleasantries and they both recalled the fun they'd shared at Tyler's farm that Sunday two weeks ago. After this, Tyler reported that Joe Vinelli had come in second in two races and third in another out in California. Then he hesitated for a few seconds. "Oh, and by the way," he said in a tone of feigned casualness. "I heard you were out in the big time last Saturday night."

"Oh—I guess—you—you mean the Charity League Dinner." Caught off guard, Zelda stammered. "Yes, what a nice affair and quite a mob of people. I guess they raised a lot of money. Were you there?" She added a stream of words while regaining her composure, hoping to pass it off lightly so Tyler wouldn't question her about it.

"No, but a couple I know, Dwight and Jean Ellington, just happened to be introduced to you that night. You see, Dwight and Mathew were fraternity brothers at the university, so they're good friends."

"I remember meeting them. He has a mustache and sort of a David Niven, British look about him. His wife was a tall, pretty blond. I believe she's the one who told me their daughter always rides in the horse show."

"That's right. That's a good description of both of them. They're nice folks, and they board Marty's horse with me. Incidently, that girl really handles her horse well. She brings home lots of blue ribbons from the shows she rides in."

Zelda was relieved that Tyler was talking about this family and their horse and not questioning why she had been there with Mathew. Yet, she was curious as to how he learned about it. "The Ellingtons were certainly friendly to me, which was nice, since I really didn't know anyone there. I'm wondering though, how in the world did they know that you knew me?" She inquired pryingly.

"They didn't. That's what makes this a curious and funny story," He chuckled. "You got time to hear it?"

"Sure, I do. With that sort of build up, I'm leery, but my curiosity gets the better of me every time."

"Well it is a story of coincidences at that. To begin with, Jean Ellington brought Marty out to the farm this afternoon after school to ride her horse and practice putting him through the horse-show routines. She does this a couple of times a week, more often when it's getting close to show time. Yesterday while Marty was riding, Jean came up to pay this month's boarding bill and to chat. She's aware that I know Mathew, so she was telling me that everyone was agog with interest when Mathew came in with this extremely pretty date that no one recognized. It created a buzz of interest, with people trying to find out who this sensational lady could be. Because, as Jean put it, we all know Mathew plays the field, but he certainly appeared to have a special interest in his intriguing new lady friend."

Zelda was glad they were on the telephone so Tyler couldn't see how flustered his words were making her feel. "That's ridiculous," Zelda protested. "She's exaggerating this whole deal."

"No, I'm sure she's not. She's certainly not exaggerating about Mathew's date being beautiful and creating a sensation."

"Well, that was nice of her to say, of course, and I love to be flattered. Who doesn't? But, honestly, she's making way too much of this. So are you," she added defiantly. "Mathew asked me to go to the dinner with him saying I'd have an opportunity there to meet a number of people who would be likely to do business with Iverson's. It really was his way of showing appreciation for my part in the Redmond estate sale. It was more of a business—courtesy sort of thing. That's all it was," she protested staunchly.

"Hey now, Zelda, I know what it was because I know Mathew. He wanted to take you because he likes being seen with you. I sure don't blame him; I like being seen with you too. It's just that dinner at the Villa Vinelli doesn't have the same social exposure as the Charity League Dinner," he said in a slightly grudging voice. The next minute he put the matter aside with sudden good humor. "Say look, I really called to tell you I've been talking to Martha."

"Martha," Her voice spiraled questioningly. "Who?"

"You know, Ernie's wife—the one who planted all those azaleas at my place."

"Oh yes," Zelda said, laughing. "That Martha."

Tyler laughed too. "Yeah, that one. And I want you to know she was really interested when I told her that you really loved her flowers, and you rather liked my horses too. In fact she was so taken by this that she insists on meeting you and she made a great suggestion."

"She did? Something colorful and horsey, no doubt." Zelda retorted, laughter underlying her words.

"You could certainly say that." Tyler chuckled, sounding genuinely amused. "You know, of course, that the Kentucky Derby is a week from Saturday at Churchill Downs over in Louisville. There is a group of about a dozen of us horsey folks here in Lexington that get together every year here at Keeneland Race Track and watch the Derby simulcast on wide screen TV. After the race we all have a picnic supper together in Paddock Park. Martha's ordered me to bring you with me, and I'm hoping you'll agree to come. How does that sound to you?"

"Totally terrific!" Zelda said with a genuine show of enthusiasm.

With this, their conversation ended on a high note. Zelda heaved a sigh of relief as she hung up the phone. She could have wished that Tyler hadn't learned that she'd gone to that dinner with Mathew, yet she guessed it was inevitable. She couldn't quite figure out what his true reaction was, however, he seemed to make fairly light of it. At least she hoped he had. She knew she was strongly attracted to Tyler, and since he was showing a good deal of interest in her, she didn't want anything to spoil that.

Chapter Seven

Time telescoped until May was rapidly moving into June. All around Wakefield Farm, wild roses, lilies of the field, and all manner of flowers were in the meadows and the pond banks were thick with rosa rugosa and honeysuckle. Following the Derby Day picnic, where she'd gotten acquainted with Martha and Ernie, Zelda had been seeing a good deal of Tyler. He took her to the Kentucky Spring Classic Horse Show, an "A" rated Hunter/Jumper show that featured top competitors from around the United States. Seeing how much she enjoyed this, two weeks later they went to the Kentucky Dressage Association's annual show in which the training of the horse and the harmony of horse and rider are judged. In between these events, Tyler also found numerous reasons to bring Zelda out to his farm. So, by the end of May, she had become quite chummy with Martha, a fact that seemed to both please and amuse Tyler.

"You and Martha have certainly hit it off well," Tyler remarked that Saturday in early June when he and Zelda were in his car driving to the Red Mile Harness Track to see the last harness race of the season. "She told me to bring you out to the farm after the race because her son has brought a car load of bedding plants and she's planning on helping you plant a couple of hanging baskets to take back to your house."

"Yes, I know. She called me about it this morning."

"Sounds like you two have found some things in common."

"You mean like flowers, horses, and you?" she teased, laughing.

He shot her a questioning glance. "How do I come into it?"

"Oh we talk about you and Ernie some—interesting and nice things, of course."

"Like what? I'd really like to hear about this. You know a guy can't help but be curious about what's being said about him. You did say it was nice, didn't you?"

Zelda nodded affirmatively, looking over at

him. She liked the slow dawning of his smile as he waited for her to tell him. "Well that very first time I met Martha, when I was helping her set out all that good food she brought to the picnic, she told me how hard you'd worked to make a success of Wakefield Farm. She said you really had to have plenty of smarts to accomplish what you did in a amazingly short time."

Tyler beamed hearing this, and his grin warmed his face like a light and caused his eyes to crinkle at the corners. "That's because I listen to Ernie, who's as smart as you can get when it comes to horses. And Martha and I both know that. He's worked with horses for nearly thirty years."

Zelda thought about Ernie with his merry blue eyes, slightly crooked nose, high, broad cheek bones, sharp angled jaw and sun-streaked, rust colored hair. "How old is he anyway?" she asked Tyler.

"Forty-eight or nine, I suppose."

"He's some older then than Martha. She just turned forty-two."

"How in the world do you know that? She's never admitted her real age to anyone. Always claims that she's twenty-five and holding. Also swears that is one of the perks you get for being a brunette, 'cause they don't age and fade like blondes."

Zelda laughed. "That sounds like something she'd pop off with. But I know she's forty-two."

"Just what makes you so sure of that?"

"Because I'm businesslike, you know," she chided him. "I simply figured it out mathematically."

"Okay, I'll bite. What's the basis for your astute calculations?" He feigned only mild interest, but there was a glint of amusement in his eyes.

"Well, she mentioned once to me that she and Ernie were married on her eighteenth birthday and that it was in May. Then another time she mentioned that their son was born a year after they were married and that he's now twenty-three. Add it up for yourself. Comes out forty-two every time."

"Sure does." He chuckled. "You know the things women talk to each other about never ceases to amaze me. So just what other interesting details did you figure out in that businesslike mind of yours?"

"No more about Martha and Ernie, but she did tell me something I didn't know about your family."

"Oh—what was that?"

Zelda felt a little hesitant for a second. Maybe she would be making a mistake to mention this to him. She didn't want to seem to be prying into his family affairs. "I was telling Martha about how I worked with my father, and that my mother had died not too long ago. She mentioned then that your father was dead and that your mother had recently sold the house where you grew up in Lexington and moved to someplace in Ohio."

"Yeah, Mom's only sister lives in Columbus. Aunt Sue is a widow too, and about a year ago she fell and broke her hip. Mom took a month's leave of absence from her job at the bank and went over to take care of Sue. Sue's been after her ever since to come live with her, and I could see it was really what my mother wanted to do." He shrugged. "I was a little apprehensive about it, but as always, Nathan stepped in to help her work things out—job wise, that is."

Puzzled, Zelda leaned forward, inclining her head toward Tyler. "Wait a minute. You're saying your mother worked at Nathan's bank here in Lexington—-right?"

Tyler nodded. "Right after Dad died, Nathan immediately saw to it that Mom was given a position at his bank that paid considerably more than she was making working in the credit department of Stebbin's Department Store. Like I told you, Nathan Redmond was our benefactor again and again," he said, a husky note in his deep voice. He paused and cleared his throat. "When Nathan learned that Mother wanted to move to be with Aunt Sue, he sent her resume and a letter of recommendation to two banks in Columbus where he had some contacts. They both offered her a position."

Tyler had readily explained all this about his mother, and now Zelda wished that he would tell her about his father. She thought about what Mathew had said about Tyler carrying around lots of emotional baggage. It struck her that his father's early death could well be a part of it. Maybe there would be an opportunity to broach the subject later, but there was no time now for they had just arrived at the Red Mile Harness Track.

The parking area was crowded with cars and mini-vans. Tyler was preoccupied with locating the closest available vacant space. After buying their tickets and getting settled in the stands, Tyler began to talk to her about today's race, giving some pointers on what to watch for, and pointing out a couple of drivers who were friends of his.

With Tyler all wound up now talking about the race, there was no possibility of her questioning him about his father's death. She crossed her arms in a gesture of resignation and followed his lead. "I guess you must come out here a lot, don't you?" she asked.

"I try to make a few races. Especially when

there's someone driving that I know. That makes it really interesting."

"Yeah, I bet it does. You know there's a charm about a harness race. At least there is to me. It always reminds me of that old classic movie *State Fair* that they still now and again show on television."

"It's an old sport all right. It appeals to all ages too," he said, a thoughtful look altering his expression. "I remember this friend of Nathan's, he was one of the more colorful fellows in harness racing around here. I'll swear, I expect he raced until he was in his early sixties. Nathan, Sara and I came out to see him race a number of times. Charlie had a lot of style, that's for sure. He held his own against the younger drivers too. You bet he did." Tyler chuckled, obviously caught up in his reminiscing, and thoroughly enjoying it.

"Sounds like quite an interesting character. What was his name?"

"Charlie Kingston. You may have seen him."

Zelda shook her head. "No, 'cause I haven't seen that many harness races. But I expect my dad's seen him. When Mother was alive they loved going to the races."

"Well, you ask your dad if he remembers the fellow who was referred to as King Charles, oldest exisiting driver at the oldest existing racetrack in the country." He cocked his head at her with an oblique look. "I bet you didn't know that fact about Red Mile Track."

"I bet I did. I know that the Red Mile is Lexington's famous racetrack, dating back to 1875. It is one of the nation's most respected harness tracks, and Standardbred racing takes place there in spring and fall." Zelda stated this glibly, a lilt in her voice and a cocky gleam in her eyes.

His eyes twinkled with warmth and humor. "You're a sharpie little show-off, you know that. Care to tell me where that canned speech came from?"

"Oh, did I fail to mention that I was a volunteer guide when Lexington celebrated the year of the horse. I led tours around to all our equine related attractions. I can tell you about the history and point out all the interesting facts, not only about Red Mile and Keeneland. And you should hear my spiel on the Kentucky Horse Park and the Horse Center." Barely able to keep the laughter from her voice, she added. "I'd be happy to give you the complete rundown right now, if you'd like to hear it."

Tyler grimaced. "Spare me that," he said emphatically.

"Okay, but you don't know what you're missing. I'm plenty good at this, and I really have it down pat," she bragged, teasing laughter shining in her eyes.

"I'll have to take your word for it," he said, laughing. "Right now, all I want you to tell me is who you're picking for me to put our two dollar bet on in the first race."

When the harness races were over, Tyler suggested that they remain in their seats and wait for the crowd to clear before going to the car. This seemed like an excellent idea to Zelda. There was presently a cooling breeze stirring because the sun had begun to lower in the sky and was now casting golden shadows as the afternoon drew to a close. It had been a fun time, and she'd enjoyed every minute. It was nice to linger a few minutes, sitting there close to Tyler. She was glad not to have to break the spell she seemed to be under lately when she was sharing these events involving horses with him. This thought made her smile and recall Martha's statements. For in the past three months, Zelda most definitely had begun to care a great deal about horses.

"While we wait, let's discuss where you'd like to go for dinner," Tyler said, interupting her silent thoughts, and at the same time laying his hand over hers. "I think we should go some place kind of different. Don't you."

Tyler's hand felt nice for he'd started gently caressing her fingers. His touch was unexpected and she found it endearing. She gave him a quick glance wondering if this was a subconscious act on his part. She rather thought it was and that he probably had no idea how his touch and his closeness disturbed her. It made a warm, fuzzy feeling flow through her that was new to her. She noticed that a faint smile curved his lips, but there was an unreadable expression in his eyes.

"So, what do you think about dinner?" He asked again.

"Oh—gee—any place is fine with me," she stammered. "Actually, I'm not very hungry now, though."

"Me either. And there is something I want us to do first. But depending on where we decide to go, I may need to make reservations, don't you think?"

She nodded. "I suppose so. However, let's pick out some place fairly casual."

"Okay, how about the River Run. They always have fresh catfish that's hard to beat."

"Yeah, and I like their shrimp Creole," she agreed with enthusiasm. "That river boat ambience is fun too, Besides, this is Saturday night so they'll have banjo music."

"Man, we can't beat that!" He stood up and pulled her to her feet. "We'll go to the River Run then, but first there's something special I want you to see. Come on," he said, taking her arm.

"Where are we going?" she asked when they were in the car driving away from Red Mile Track.

"We're going to the farm," he said, giving her a non-committal smile.

"To do what?"

"I can't tell you."

Totally intrigued, Zelda's curiosity was starting to get the best of her. "Why not?" she demanded petulantly.

"I have to show you, that's why. It's something I want you to see for yourself. To be honest I really want to see how long it takes for you to notice what's occurred, and naturally I want to see your reaction." He followed his puzzling words with an enigmatic smile.

This made Zelda feel rather uneasy. She eyed him questioningly. "What are you up to? Are you putting me to some kind of test? Is that what all this is leading up to?"

"No, I'm just curious to see how observant you are."

"Sounds like a test to me," she said, her dark eyebrows pulled into an affronted frown. "And what if I flunk? Are you going to banish me from Wakefield Farm forever."

"Absolutely not. Nothing that drastic. In fact, exactly the opposite, you'd have to spend more quality time there with me so you'd pick up on every nuance and change as it takes place."

Zelda threw up her hands. "You've got me totally baffled, Tyler. First you say you have something to show me. Then in the second breath you imply that I may not be observant enough to see it. Sounds like a no-win situation to me. Call me a poor sport, but I don't like the odds."

"Hey, it's not like that, honest." He reached over and gave her an affectionate pat on the arm. "There's just been this new development that I want to share with you. Humor me and play along with this. Can't you?"

Tyler seemed so intent on this that she felt trapped like a moth in a jar. "I guess I can," she answered half-heartedly.

A half hour later, Tyler and Zelda were at his farm walking leisurely toward the nearest paddock. The path they took was dappled with the afternoon sunlight and a light breeze rippled through the blue grass. High above the massive oak trees, a red-tailed hawk had set his wings against the wind and was sailing lazily along the air currents.

"How serene and tranquil it seems here now. Is that because of the time of day or because it's summer?" Zelda asked as she rested her arms on the top rail of the fence and gazed at Sweet Dream who was grazing nearby in the paddock.

"A little of both I think," Tyler answered.

"Where is Dream Maker? I don't see him. Surely he wouldn't stay in the barn by himself, would he?" she asked, a questioning frown giving her a worried expression. "Nothing is wrong with him I hope. Don't tell me that all your talk about showing me something was because something has happened to Dream Maker." Zelda's voice became more agitated with each word.

Tyler quickly shook his head. "He's fine. In the pink in fact. He's just getting old enough to break away from his mother." Tyler chuckled. "He's a confident young rascal. Come on, I'll show you." Tyler pulled her away from the fence and looping his arm through hers, he led her off toward the southern pasture.

When they reached the paddock beyond the second barn, Zelda counted half a dozen or more horses roaming around the perimeters while a trio of sorrel colored mares and one black gelding stood in the shade of a rounded, spreading chestnut tree. At first she couldn't find Dream Maker, but a minute later she caught sight of him trotting toward the side of the paddock fence where she and Tyler stood. "He looks quite a bit different from the last time I saw him," she said, leaning on the top rail and studying the young horse as he drew closer.

Tyler moved close beside her. "Different how? Tell me what changes you see?" He leaned his arms on the railing and scrutinized Zelda closely as she eyed the colt she'd named and developed such a fondness for.

"Well, he's taller for one thing—and smoother, somehow. He used to be sort of fuzzy looking. Now he's sleek with that touch of class you breeders talk about in your thoroughbreds." She made a little clicking sound to underline her words.

Tyler chuckled. "Fuzzy huh—well that's a pretty apt assessment." He sounded amused, but pleased with her statement. "I'm impressed that you noticed that he's been spruced up a bit. He's had a little trim, and his ears and feet clipped."

"Like I said, makes him look sharp. So now that I didn't flunk your show and tell test, I want you to tell me what else has been happening to him. And don't leave out a single detail."

He nodded. "First, it was becoming apparent that it was time to wean him away from Sweet Dream and start him getting used to being around a number of other horses. So we moved him into this other pasture and it didn't take him long to adapt to the change. Actually he was fairly calm and confident with the other horses after the first week, but Ernie and I intend to move slow with him. Ernie has helped me to understand that the correct approach to one horse may be totally wrong for another. You have to look at a horse as an individual, get to really know and understand him, then you take what steps are necessary for that particular horse's needs."

"You'll do it right with Dream Maker. I'm sure of that."

"We'll all do it right and we'll do it together," Tyler said, placing his arm around her shoulders and hugging her. "You are a part of this dream making too, you know."

He had been watching her with intelligence and interest, and how as he said this, his eyes were gentle and he smiled. She could tell by the tone of his voice that he meant it and suddenly she felt a warm glow flow through her. Maybe it was just the late afternoon sunshine and the heat coming from the nearby horses, but she knew as she looked at Tyler that it was more than that. It was the curve of his mouth, the tender expression in his eyes, and the sensitivity of the things he had said. Then, the following moment, he kissed her slowly. It was a kiss that said more than a thousand words. It was a magic moment, a moment when the truth became clear to Zelda. What was between her and Tyler was more than just an innocent romance. It was something deep and real and special.

Chapter Eight

Zelda was humming to herself as she stood at the counter in the kitchen cracking eggs into a bowl to make an omelet for her father's breakfast. The fluorescent lights were on overhead and in the inset beneath the oak grain cabinets, illuminating the brick floor, the white and blue fleur-de-lis tiling at the back of the counter, and the copper pots hanging neatly above the stove on their wrought-iron hooks. She tried to identify the familiar melody issuing automatically from her throat. She thought it might be the love song that was sung in the movie *The Horse Whisperer* which she and Tyler had watched on tape last night along with Joe Vinelli and his current girl-

95

friend. She was still speculating on this when her dad joined her in the kitchen.

"My, my, to what do I owe your special Sunday ham and cheese omelet breakfast when this is a weekday cereal, toast and coffee morning?" Claude Iverson greeted his daughter with a broad smile as he watched her adding milk to the eggs and beating them lightly with a wire whip. "I think you may be so smitten with that good looking horseman of yours that you don't know what day it is." He teased her with a knowing look. "Am I right about that?"

"I'll admit to being somewhat smitten, as you say." She wrinkled her nose at him as she added the ham and seasonings to the egg mixture and poured it all into the omelet pan. "However, I'm quite well aware that it's Thursday, the twenty second of July, which is the day you are flying to Denver to visit your brother, Frank. As for my giving you a hearty breakfast, that's because your plane leaves at ten-forty this morning and they'll only give you a soft drink and a few peanuts in flight. Uncle Frank will pick you up in Denver and drive you forty some miles into the mountains before you will get anything like a regular meal."

"You're probably right. And Frank promised that Barbara was cooking fresh rainbow trout for dinner tonight, so I'll be good and hungry to do justice to her great cooking." He opened the refrigerator and poured himself a glass of orange juice. "Barbara always cooks up a storm on my yearly visits with them. When I come back in two weeks you may have to roll me off the plane," he added, as he sat down at the kitchen table and began to drink his juice.

"A couple of extra pounds would look good on you, Dad. So just eat up and enjoy yourself."

"I'll do that all right."

Zelda added the grated cheese to the omelet and then flipped it over. She had already set the table, and she'd been drinking her juice while she cooked. Now she poured two mugs of coffee and then served up the omelet, giving the largest portion to her father.

"You know I think I chose just the right time to be gone," her dad said, as he picked up his fork and began to eat. "We have no estate sales this month and the only one scheduled for August is not until the last of the month. I'll be back in plenty of time to prepare for that. Hm—hm, this is delicious," he told her as he paused to take another bite. "You've got the July consignment sale to handle without me, but Carrie Lee can be of some help to you. And I suggest you see if that friend of yours that works part time at the Lexington Antique Gallery can come and work with you at least on the first day, second too if you'd like to have her. She's knowledgeable and she strikes up a good rapport with the customers."

Zelda nodded. "You're talking about Sherrie Anderson. You're right too, she's as cordial as an open door. I think I will see if she can work a couple of days. Our sale coincides with the Charity League Horse show and you know that's apt to pull in a large group of interested buyers from outside Lexington."

"Say, speaking of the Charity League show, that reminds me. Mathew Redmond dropped off a letter for you last night when you were gone. He said it was an invitation to some party in connection with the horse show. Said he'd call you about it this morning." Claude frowned. "I swear I don't remember what I did with it now. I expect I either laid it on the hall table or carried it in and put it on top of the stereo. I'll go look for it right now." He pushed back his chair and started to stand up.

"No, don't get up," Zelda said quickly. "Finish your breakfast. I'll find it later. It's nothing I have to see right this minute." She shrugged, passing the matter off with feigned indifference. The fact was that she had hoped by this time that Mathew would have forgotten about Gloria Sandefur asking him to bring her to this party she and her husband were having during the horse show. Zelda couldn't imagine that Mathew would even want to take her to it now. After all, she had rebuffed his attentions toward her, they had never really dated, and there was no way anyone could see them as a couple. Surely it would be a relief to both of them if she bowed out of the Sandefur party. Wouldn't it?

"Say, suddenly you're looking as dismal as a wet Derby Day. Have you got something on your mind you haven't told me about?"

Her father's voice broke into Zelda's disquieting thoughts. She forced a quick smile and jumped up from the table. "The only thing on my mind is pouring you another cup of coffee," she said brightly. "And how I'm looking is not dismal, but wistful. And that's because I shall miss having breakfast with you for these next two weeks, but I'm happy because I know you're going to have a great vacation in Colorado."

Claude arched his eyebrows at her, giving her his discerning, fatherly look. "I think you are artfully dodging the issue," he said. "Yet on the other hand, that was a mighty pretty speech and I appreciate it." He smiled warmly and handed her his cup. "Now, let's have that second cup of coffee and then you can drive me to the airport."

It was the middle of the afternoon when Mathew telephoned her. "Did you see your invitation from Gloria Sandefur?" he asked without any preliminaries.

"Yes, Dad remembered to give it to me this morning as I was getting ready to take him out to catch a plane for Denver," she explained, matter of factly.

"Gloria said she hoped you wouldn't mind her sending your invitation in with mine, but she hesitated to send it to your business place and she said she didn't have your home address. She wanted me to be sure and tell you that she's looking forward to seeing you again."

"That's nice of her and I appreciate the invitation."

"I hope you hadn't forgotten that I'm to take you to her party." Mathew's voice was smooth, but insistent.

Zelda hesitated, not knowing just what she wanted to say. "Actually, I had almost forgotten about it. To be perfectly honest, I feel peculiar about the whole thing. Gloria Sandefur scarcely knows me, and I really feel I'd like to back out of it, if that's all right with you."

"No, it's not all right with me. I've counted on our attending this party together. I'll be highly disappointed if you don't let me take you." His silky voice held a challenge. "Besides, my Aunt Rosalind is coming for the horse show. She and Gloria are long-time friends, so she'll be at the party and I think you'll enjoy meeting her. She told Dad on the phone that you'd arranged for pictures of Sara that were found in my grandfather's house to be sent to her. She'd like the chance to thank you for your part in this."

Mathew's lengthy spiel captured Zelda's interest. She was curious about a lot of things relating to Rosalind and Sara. The opportunity of meeting and talking to Rosalind was highly tempting. "I'd enjoy the opportunity of seeing her too, of course. I just had thought that because you'd mentioned this party to me a month or so ago, you now felt obligated, and I wanted to give you a chance to change your mind," she countered smoothly. "But it's very nice of you to still wish to take me, and I'd be delighted to be with you," she said, planting a smile in her voice.

"Well now, that's more like it. I'm glad we're doing this, Zelda. And there's no doubt in my mind that it will turn out to be a rather interesting evening all the way around."

Zelda thought there was an innuendo in his words. Disturbed, she frowned wondering what he meant by *all the way around*. Their conversation ended. Zelda said good-bye, but as she hung up the phone she had an uneasy feeling that she was going to regret her decision to attend this party with Mathew.

* * *

In July the evenings are long and lingering. After the sky darkens the moon soars slowly through the branches of the trees and then sails unencumbered into the indigo heavens attended by the shining stars. The Sandefur party was held on just that kind of radiant July night.

Though the evening air was balmy, there was enough of a light breeze stirring to make it pleasant. Zelda had hoped that they would arrive promptly, but Mathew was one for making a bit of an entrance. So it turned out that they were one of the last three couples to join what appeared to be a gathering of perhaps seventy-five people.

Apparently, Mathew was acquainted with most of the guests, and soon he and Zelda were mingling about, talking with friends, as they sipped a mint julep. After a while, several of Mathew's friends suggested that they all get their food and find a place to eat together. They then went into the dining room where an elongated mahogany dining table was laden with an elaborate supper buffet. There were "oh's" and "ah's" from everyone as they admired this beautiful display of delicious food.

"I'm told there are lots of tables set up outside," one of the fellows announced as they moved around the table filling their plates. "I'll go grab one for us and you all follow along."

His announcement made Zelda aware that the music she'd heard coming from beyond the spacious rooms of the house was a sign that this gala party was more extensive than she'd thought. As she and Mathew passed through French doors out onto the terrace, she saw that there were half as many guests in the garden as were inside the house. The music that she'd heard came from a five piece orchestra located at the far end of a wide brick patio. A temporary wooden floor had been laid over a section of the patio and several couples were dancing.

Zelda angled her head close to Mathew's. "This whole set up is absolutely fabulous," she told him in a stage whisper.

"Yeah, quite a posh affair," he agreed. "Aren't you glad you came?"

"Of course, I am." She smiled. "And I'm counting on getting to see Rosalind too. Have you seen her here?"

"Not yet, but I'm not surprised. Knowing her, I'm sure she got here and cornered some of her old buddies. They're probably gathered at a table in a corner of the garden gabbing away. I'll go hunt her up after we've eaten," he assured her as he steered her toward the table where his group of friends were now gathering.

Later when they'd finished supper, several of the couples got up to dance. At that time Mathew and Zelda excused themselves to go look for Rosalind. They circled all around the terrace before wandering slowly through the garden.

"There's Rosalind," Mathew cried suddenly. "Standing over there talking with the Sandefur's."

Zelda looked in the direction Mathew had indicated. "You mean that woman standing between two men with their backs to us."

"Right, the blonde in that odd kind of greenish colored dress."

Zelda had to smile at a man's description of what looked to Zelda from this distance to be a lovely shade of aquamarine, which is a most becoming color for blonds. "It looks more blue than green to me, and very pretty I might add," she said, laughing.

"Whatever," he grumbled, grabbing her arm. "Come on. Let's go get her."

They were about thirty feet from where Rosalind stood, and it took them a few minutes to wind though the tables to reach her. Since Rosalind had her back to them, Zelda could only tell that she was tall and slender. At that moment, another couple joined the group, and Rosalind and the man on her right started to leave to give the newcomers a chance to talk with their host and hostess.

"Roz, wait a minute," Mathew called out, hurrying to catch up to her.

Rosalind turned around. "Why Mathew," she said. "I've been hoping we'd run into you." As she spoke, the man with her also turned.

Zelda caught her breath in surprise. "Tyler— I didn't know you were coming here tonight. I mean, I didn't expect to know anyone—so seeing you is a nice surprise." She knew she was babbling, but the words poured out of her mouth without her volition. Having said them, she flushed with embarrassment from making such inane remarks.

"I think we both have the same reaction at seeing each other," Tyler said in a strained tone of voice, his eyes regarding her with searching gravity.

"Roz, this is Zelda Iverson," Mathew interjected imperiously. "As I'm sure my dad has told you, Zelda is my talented friend who handled Grandfather's estate sale so capably for us. Also, I believe she located some pictures of Sara for you."

Rosalind was obviously confused by the situation. She shot a questioning look at Tyler, a perplexed expression on her face as she seemed to size up what was going on between Tyler, Zelda, and her nephew. "Well, I'm so glad to have this chance to meet you, Zelda," she said, with a gracious smile. "Your company certainly did a successful sale for our family. Barton tells me that you sold everything but a few outdated books on banking and finance. I think you all are miracle workers," she laughed. "I don't think my dad ever threw away anything. So how you managed to dispose of it all is amazing."

Her words gratified Zelda and helped her regain a bit of composure. "Your father owned countless treasures, and his was a most interesting and rewarding estate sale to handle. I'm just glad you and Barton were so pleased."

"Well, honey, I've said it before and I'll say it again," Mathew said, placing his arm around Zelda's shoulders. "You went the whole nine yards and did ol' Grandpa Nathan's sale up brown."

Zelda passed his words off with a shrug, and tried to inch away from him. She sensed that his hugging her shoulders and calling her "honey" was all calculated to annoy Tyler. Glancing at Tyler and seeing the frown that lined his brow and the tense thrust of his jaw, she could tell Mathew's proprietary manner had clearly done just that.

Zelda felt that Rosalind had noticed Tyler's reactions too, for she immediately took over the conversation again. "And about the pictures of Sara," she said, turning her full attention again to Zelda. "Tyler told me that you discovered them and I want you to know how much I appreciate you and Tyler collaborating to see that they got sent to me."

It was Mathew's time to scowl. "I didn't know you had any part in that Tyler. 'Course, you've always been a big help in everything where Sara or Roz was concerned. The proverbial white knight to Redmond ladies in distress," he scoffed.

"No big deal on my part," Tyler said, passing it off with a shrug. "I simply happened to be at the estate sale when Zelda inventoried a box of pictures and some of Nathan's memorabilia. Noticing Sara's photos with Sweet Dream, I mentioned to Zelda that I knew Rosalind would want to have them, and I offered to take care of sending them to her. Just doing a small favor for my old friend Rosalind and my new friend Zelda," Tyler said, a flash of humor crossing his face.

Mathew's expression was one of pained tolerance that did not entirely hide his resentment of Tyler. "Well, I'm sure, Roz, that you have a lot of friends to look up here tonight, so Zelda and I will head off to enjoy some dancing." With this, he immediately took a firm hold of Zelda's hand and began to back away.

Tyler's eyes caught and held hers a moment. "See you, Zelda," he said in a deep tone.

His voice echoed her own longings. "Yes," she murmured, nodding her head. The following second Mathew tugged on her hand forcing her to turn away. All animation had now faded from Zelda's face. She was quiet, withdrawn, and worried. Aching with an inner pain, she could only wish with all her heart that this night had never been.

Chapter Nine

Zelda's thoughts and emotions were jumbled in a crazy quilt of disorder. Seeing Tyler tonight with Rosalind Trask raised questions in her mind—and as she contemplated these questions, the answers she came up with filled her with despair. Logic told her that Tyler was not acquainted with the Sandefurs, it was Rosalind who was a close friend of Gloria's. Therefore, she obviously had asked Tyler to escort her to the party. Certainly he would be only too happy to be with her—and why not? He had a genuine affection for her. She was his benefactor's daughter, more important than that, she was Sara's mother. And hadn't Tyler been in love with Sara? Certainly from everything she'd seen and heard, Sara loved and idolized him. And why shouldn't she? Tyler had altered her life. He'd worked with her and helped her from the time she was a teenager. He'd made her dream come true by helping her become a confident and capable horsewoman.

Momentarily distracted by hearing the antique wall clock in the upstairs hall chime and strike the late hour of one, she undressed and climbed into bed. She closed her eyes, willing herself to fall asleep. Try as she would, her tired mind continued to talk endlessly to itself.

What if Sara had wanted to marry Tyler? Couldn't that be the reason Nathan had been so eager to see that Tyler owned his own horse farm. Nathan would want Tyler to be successful so he could provide a secure and comfortable life for Sara. That made sense. Yet, hadn't Tyler said that Nathan had been a benefactor to his family as well as to him? He'd provided Tyler's mother with a better paying job after Tyler's father died, and she remembered that Tyler said Nathan had also seen to it that his mother had good job opportunities offered to her when she left Lexington to live with her sister. So his help and interest in Tyler and his family began even before the time that Tyler began working with Sara and her horse. So at least in the beginning, it was not all about Sara and it continued on after Sara's death.

So was that the emotional baggage Mathew had hinted that Tyler carried with him? Was his life tied to the past because of all Nathan had done for him? And most of all, was Tyler so emotionally enmeshed in his feelings for Sara that there was no room in his heart for another love? This last was the question that she needed to have answered. For if that was the case, then she had to put him out of her life before she fell more in love with him than she already was.

The rest of the night, Zelda's mind mumbled these thoughts until finally, sleep crumbled like an old wall and buried the sounds.

In no time at all, it seemed the first pale shafts of dawn lightened the sky. The night had passed and Zelda felt as if she had scarcely slept at all. She stirred, stretched, and sighed wearily. At the same time telling herself she had to get up and get going. This was Saturday and the second day of Iverson's summer consignment sale. With a lot of out–of–towners here for the horse show, business should be brisk. She was counting on a record number of sales, and to achieve this, she challenged herself to focus on the business at hand and banish all other thoughts and emotions from her mind.

Zelda's determination spurred her on. She got up out of bed, took an invigorating shower, artfully applied some subtle make-up to camouflage

her sleepless night. Then once she donned a becoming yellow and white linen dress, she looked
at her reflection in the mirror and decided even
if she didn't look as fresh as a just-picked daisy,
she looked at least as good as a day-old one.

Soon after Zelda got to the shop, Sherrie Anderson joined her. The two of them got the lights
turned on in the display cases and shifted a collection of Dresden figurines to a more prominent
area. Zelda had expected this group to sell early
and had been surprised that only one small piece
had sold the first day of the sale. "I think this
Dresden may be a bit over-priced. What do you
think, Sherrie?"

"The price isn't really out of line for the quality," Sherrie said. "I think, however, we'd have
a greater show of interest if you could cut the
price by ten percent."

"Good point," Zelda readily agreed. "I'll retag
them, and who knows, we may get a collector
who'll buy the whole lot." She gave Sherrie an
optimistic smile.

Carrie Lee arrived while Zelda was making
the price changes, and the three of them had
everything ready when they opened the doors at
ten o'clock.

Soon after, the first customers came in, four
women together and shortly after them a couple,

the Harrington's, who were regulars at Iverson's sales. Zelda greeted them cordially, and when an antique, Chinese teakwood screen caught their interest, she promptly turned them over to Sherrie, who related the history of the screen and pointed out the intricacies of the design.

One of the women from the group of four asked Zelda if she had any Victorian parlor chairs or antique tables with marble tops. Zelda led her into another room where there were a number of both rosewood and walnut chairs, setees, tables, and commodes circa 1840 to 1890. Less than an hour later the woman had decided on a pair of walnut chairs and an oval side table in rosewood with a bevel-edged marble top.

This sale was exactly what Zelda needed to brighten her day. Revitalized, she returned to the front gallery, where she was both surprised and pleased to find Rosalind Trask admiring the Dresden collection.

"Good morning!" She greeted her with enthusiasm, hurrying over to where Rosalind stood. "I didn't expect to see anybody from last night's big party in here before midafternoon.

"Well, I'll admit it was a bit hard to get my middle-aged bones up and going this morning," she said, a sparkle lighting her gray-green eyes and a genial smile marking her patrician face. "But there was method in my madness, Zelda."

She added, "You see, Tyler told me about this big summer sale of yours last night after I'd met you. He even showed me your ad in the newspaper that mentioned a signed Ralph Barber paperweight made in Millville, New Jersey." Her voice rose mirroring her excitement. "So you see, I couldn't miss a chance to add a Ralph Barber to my collection. I just have my fingers crossed that you haven't sold it." She held up her hands with both her index and third fingers crossed. "You haven't, have you?" she asked.

"I'm not sure. We had three Millville paperweights on consignment, but only one was a signed Barber. One sold yesterday and I'm not sure which one. Come with me and let's have a look."

Zelda led Rosalind across the gallery to a display case. She glanced at the contents as she slipped behind to unlock the case. "No, it's still here," she announced, immediately taking it out and placing it on top of the case.

Rosalind gazed at it in wonder, a look of sheer elation on her attractive face. "Oh, I can't believe it. Isn't this the one they call the Millville Rose."

Zelda nodded. "Yes, it's the yellow rose on a footed base. Ralph Barber was a perfectionist you know, and this is perhaps his best. It's a choice piece."

Rosalind had picked up the paperweight and

was examining it closely. "It's in mint condition, not a scratch on it." She paused, a questioning look on her face. "I hope you won't mind my out-of-state check. I simply must have this."

"Your check is just fine, of course," Zelda assured her, reaching under the display case for tissue paper.

While Rosalind made out her check, Zelda carefully wrapped the Millville Rose in two layers of paper and then placed it in a black, drawstring plastic bag that had Iversons emblazoned on it in white block letters.

"I know you have customers to take care of, Zelda, but I wonder if you could spare me a few more minutes," Rosalind asked, as Zelda handed her the paperweight she'd purchased. "I wanted to talk to you about something important, and ask a favor of you, if I could."

"Of course, you can. What do you say we go back to the office. No one will bother us there. Better yet, we can sit down." She gave a little laugh. "I don't know about you, but after that big party last night, I'm tired. I plan to grab every chance I can today to get off my feet."

As Zelda led Rosalind to the office at the back of the shop, she was filled with curiosity about what the important thing Rosalind wished to talk about might be. Did it have something to do with Tyler? She guessed that it might, but hoped that it didn't. She had enough unsettling thoughts re-garding Tyler to worry her already. At this time, she felt helpless to cope with anything more. As for the favor Rosalind wanted, the only thing Zelda figured she could possibly do for her would be to scout out an exceptional antique pa-perweight or two for her collection. She chewed the corner of her lip thoughtfully as she won-dered if, indeed, that might be it.

The office they now entered was of modest size, actually just large enough for a nineteeth century carved wooden desk, two file cabinets, some built-in book shelves with cabinets below, and a pair of mahogany arm chairs with U-shaped backs and upholstered wine colored leather seats.

"I'll get right to the point," Rosalind said, as she sat down in one of the chairs. "Tyler told me that you are the one who gave Dream Maker his name. Incidently, it's a glorious name. I love it," she added with genuine enthusiasm.

"Well it did seem a fitting name for a colt of Sweet Dream's. Tyler has great hopes for him too. I'm sure he's told you."

Rosalind nodded. "You and I share those high hopes and fine dreams with him, don't we." She said it not as a question, but as a statement of fact. "Now Tyler told me something else that I need to talk to you about," she continued. "It's that box he bought that had Sara's pictures and that old horse-shoe." Her voice now held a wistful note. "I'm afraid I'm a bit sentimental when it comes to Sara's horse," she said with a sigh.

"Of course you are—and Tyler is too. You should have seen how pleased he was when he discovered that horseshoe. He told me he remembered the day Sweet Dream threw that shoe."

"Those were the happy times for Sara. Her father and I cherish those memories." Rosalind's eyes were misty and pensive, and she leaned forward, looking intently at Zelda. "And that brings me to the favor I wish to ask of you, Zelda. "Do you recall the cash money that was also in that box with Sara's photos."

Rosalind mentioning those bills wrapped up in a sheet of paper took Zelda by surprise. "Why— why yes, of course, I do. I returned them to your brother exactly as I found them," she explained, looking puzzled and feeling a bit uneasy.

"Yes, I know. Barton told me that, and he promptly gave the money back to me."

"Then it did belong to you. Tyler guessed that the *R* on the note stood for either Rosalind or Redmond. He also even speculated that it could be the repayment of a debt someone owed Nathan. It proved an interesting mystery, finding cash money in that box of old papers and memorabilia of Nathan's." Zelda shrugged. "I'm glad our little mystery is now solved," she added, with a light laugh.

"Only somewhat solved, Zelda," Rosalind told her, with an enigmatic smile. "You see, though I sent those bills to my father, they actually were Sara's. She'd saved them up and wanted them used for a particular purpose, something she wanted to do for Tyler when the right time came. That's the reason when Sara died that I sent the money to my father. He was here in Lexington keeping in touch with Tyler, so he'd know when the time was right, and would take care of doing what Sara wanted."

Zelda frowned. "But Nathan is gone now too."

"Exactly. And that's why I need you, Zelda." She reached over and patted Zelda's hand. "You see, I live a good part of the year in Portugal and I really need help from someone right here in Lexington who's in touch with Tyler and knows what's happening with him. And I'm sure you're aware that neither Barton nor Mathew has a friendly word for Tyler, much less even the slightest inclination to perform a favor for me that has anything to do with Tyler Wakefield," she said, and there was a slight bitterness in her tone of voice.

"Naturally, I have noticed that Mathew and Tyler weren't all that friendly," Zelda said. She felt somewhat hesitant about prodding Rosalind about the animosity between Tyler and Mathew. Yet she was curious, and Rosalind had brought it up. She took a deep breath and plunged in. "What's the problem there? Tyler was such great friends with Nathan and you and Sara. Why should Mathew and Barton not be friends with him too?"

Rosalind shrugged. "Mainly, I think there's some resentment there. You know of course that my father was keen on seeing that Tyler could complete his education after his father died. And he was also determined to help make it possible for Tyler to have his own horse farm. In short, he intended to do all the things Tyler's father would have tried to do for him if he'd lived. My father felt responsible for Tyler in some ways, and I'm sure Mathew was jealous of the time and interest his grandfather gave to Tyler."

"Oh I can see how there might have been a little rivalry between them when they were young and still in college. But now that Nathan is gone and both of them are successful in their chosen careers, they should stop trying to annoy each other." Zelda made an amused face. "Men are so obvious. At least we women employ subtle hostility"

Rosalind snickered. "I'll say this, last night when Mathew brought you over to talk to Tyler

and me, his every word and gesture was calculated to bother Tyler. Mathew was as blatant as
a circus parade." She chuckled and shook her
head. "So you can understand why I'm asking
you to handle this for me."

"I'll be glad to help anyway I can. Just what
is it I'm to do?"

Rosalind opened her hand bag and drew out
an envelope. "Here's Sara's money," she said,
handing it to Zelda. "I want you to keep it until
the time Tyler has Dream Maker trained and
ready for his first stakes race."

Zelda looked bemused. "But that's gonna be
a long time off. Why, thoroughbreds aren't
trained on the track until they're classified as two
year olds. At least I know that Tyler and Ernie
believe Dream Maker shouldn't be trained at too
early an age."

"I know, but that's why you will pick the right
time. Because when Dream Maker is coming
close to running his first race, that will be the
time to tell Tyler that Sara is giving him his
silks."

"His silks—what do you mean?" Zelda inquired, curiously."

"Oh you know, the color and design of the
shirt and cap the jockey wears identifies the
horse's owner. It's like a coat of arms. The silks
identify Tyler and Wakefield Farms at the track.

So when the time comes, you talk to Tyler, ask him to choose the two colors he wants, and then you order the silks from one of the commercial firms that make silks. I've enclosed the name of two that are widely used by the race horse owners in and around Lexington. It shouldn't be much trouble."

"No trouble at all," Zelda exclaimed, enthusiastically. It's going to be such fun to have a part in it." I can just imagine how pleased Tyler will be to know Sara wanted to do this for him."

"It's a small thing, but it was something she could do on her own for all that Tyler had done for her." Rosalind said, and there was a catch in her voice and a film of tears clouded her eyes.

"Believe me, it'll be no small thing to Tyler," Zelda assured her in a sympathetic voice. Both Nathan and Sara are a memorable part of his life. I'm sure you know that. He says Nathan was his benefactor and he's forever indebted to him."

"That indebtedness goes both ways Zelda. My father would be the first one to tell you that." Rosalind made this surprising statement with quiet emphasis.

Zelda stared at her in amazement. "What do you mean?" She shook her head. "I don't understand."

"It's sort of involved, and it's a story I'm sure Tyler will want to tell you one of these days.

Now I've kept you from your work long enough," she said, changing the subject. She stood up quickly then. "Thank you so much Zelda. I appreciate your helping me." She smiled warmly, gave Zelda a motherly pat on her shoulder, and then was gone.

Chapter Ten

So Mathew wasn't the only one who made cryptic remarks about Tyler's involvement with the Redmond family. Rosalind now was intimating that although her father had indeed been Tyler's benefactor, still on the other hand, and for some obscure reason, Nathan was in Tyler's debt. She would truly like to know the story behind this, she thought heaving a sigh. She wondered if as Rosalind had said, that Tyler would want to tell her about it. As she left the office to get back to work, she vowed to herself that if Tyler didn't explain all this soon, she darn well was going to ask him point blank what Rosalind had been referring to.

It was well after six o'clock that evening when

Zelda closed up shop and headed for home. It was warm outside with only the faintest stirring of a breeze. Low on the western horizon, the glow of the sinking sun tinted a thin layer of clouds with soft shades of coral and purple.

As she wheeled into her driveway and parked, she was amazed to see Tyler sitting on the front porch steps. He was hunched slightly forward with his forearms on his knees and his hands clasped as though he was deep in thought. The second she got out of the car, he stood up and came hurrying toward her.

Her heart raced with joy at finding him at her house, obviously waiting for her. It was totally preposterous, but she had a crazy urge to run to him and hurl herself into his arms. She didn't, of course. Instead she raised her hand. "Hi there," she said, greeting him with a radiant smile. "What's up?"

Tyler grinned, relief etched on his face. Instantly he enclosed her hand in his so that her fingers were exposed, rubbing them against his jaw in a loving gesture. "I was getting worried that you weren't coming home." He smiled down at her, and his voice was smoky soft while the allure in his eyes almost took her breath away.

"Because of the sale we're having, it took me awhile to close up." She explained as they walked to her front door. "Besides, I had no idea you'd be here."

"I guess I should have called. I wanted to see you so much though that I just came."

"It's fine. I'm glad you're here."

"I hoped I could take you to dinner, if you're free."

"I'm free as a bird," she quipped, taking out her key and unlocking the front door.

"Swell, just tell me where you'd like to go and I'll go in right now and call for a reservation." His mood seemed suddenly buoyant.

"Golly, Tyler," she said, frowning. "I don't know about this. It's Saturday night, and I bet anything it'll be eight o'clock or later before we could get a reservation at most places." She gave a weary sigh. "After that blow-out party last night and then working all day, I'm just not up to the hassle of going out. What do you say we stay right here and eat?"

Tyler's face brightened at her suggestion. "Sure, that sounds great to me. I'll call and order pizza, or I can run get us Chinese carry-out. Whichever you'd prefer."

"I've got a better idea. How about if I fix my dad's favorite meal for us—chicken-fried steak with cream gravy?"

His brows lifted in amazement. "You know

how to make honest to goodness cream gravy?" he asked, his eyes lighting up with interest.

"Sure do, best you ever tasted," she bragged, tossing her head up and looking at him with a gleeful twinkle in her eyes. "Some of us business types do find time for other things than work, you know."

"I'm beginning to find that out." He smiled that easy smile of his. "And believe me, honey, chicken-fried steak and cream gravy is a sure way to a man's heart. So take me, I'm yours," he declared, holding out his arms to her with a sparkle now in his eyes and his smile.

Zelda felt her heartbeat throb in her ears. She cleared her throat, pretending not to be affected by the innuendo in Tyler's playful words. "Watch out, Tyler! Better not get yourself out on a limb. I must warn you that what I cook isn't as fancy as what you're used to at Vinelli's."

"Vinelli's is great, and they do serve some mighty fine Italian dishes, but I'll choose good, simple American fare right here with you over Vinelli's any day," he said, circling his outstretched arms around her waist. "To have you sitting across the dining table from me makes the meal special for me. The key ingredient is you, Zelda," he said as he kissed the tip of her nose.

"Sweet talk like that will earn you a chocolate sundae for your dessert," she murmured, her lips curving in a tremulous smile. She eased away from him then and steered him to the kitchen. "Now, here's the plan," she said, turning on the ceiling fan and pointing to the refrigerator. "There are cans of iced tea, cokes, and lemon-lime drinks in there. So help yourself while I go change my clothes." She turned and started out of the kitchen. "I won't be more than ten minutes," she called back over her shoulder.

When Zelda returned she was wearing jeans, a sky-blue tee, and a pair of matching blue tennis shoes. "Well now, you look neat and ready to go to work," Tyler said, giving her the once over and beaming with approval.

"Yep, I sure am," she announced, as she opened one of the kitchen cabinets next to the stove and removed two sauce pans and a skillet. She then went to the fridge and took out two potatoes from the vegetable bin and the package of minute steaks from the freezer top. She then handed the potatoes to Tyler along with a peeler and one of the pans. "This dinner is going to be a cooperative venture. I need you to peel and quarter these potatoes. You can't have chicken fried steak without mashed potatoes you know."

"No, of course not," Tyler agreed, downing the last swallow from the cola can and heading to the sink to perform his assigned task. "It may surprise you to know that I not only know how to boil potatoes to the right degree of doneness, but I also know how much salt, milk and butter to add to mash them to perfection." he said, cocking his head and grinning.

She smiled back at him. "Good! Then the mashed potatoes are your department. But once you've got them ready to cook, I've one more thing for you to do while I fix the meat."

"Just name it."

"I want you to look through the pantry shelves and pick out a can of vegetables that you'd like for dinner," she said, gesturing toward a tall cabinet door at the far side of the kitchen. "There's quite a variety, corn, beets, beans, tomatoes, peas, even sauerkraut. You name it, we have it."

"Man, you do have a big selection here," Tyler agreed, a few minutes later when he pulled open the cabinet door and inspected the contents of the four various shelves. He reached in and chose a can. "I'm taking green beans."

"Good. There's a can opener in the drawer next to the sink."

They both now concentrated on their assigned tasks, and in a relatively short time, they were seated across the table from each other enjoying the home cooked meal they'd created together, and conversing amiably about the day's events.

"Oh, I want to thank you, Tyler, for telling Rosalind about our consignment sale. She came in this morning and bought a really lovely paperweight for her collection."

"Hey, that's neat." He sounded pleased. "I knew she'd find something interesting to buy. Besides that, she told me she was eager to check out the beautiful gal I allowed to pick out the name for my high-hopes horse," he told her, his eyes twinkling with warmth and humor. "You see, this was a singularly significant act on my part," he added, in a lower, huskier tone. Then his gaze met hers and she found herself staring into hazel eyes that had gone serious.

The idea of what he'd said sent her spirits soaring. She was lost in dreamy thoughts for a moment. It took a few seconds for her to focus her mind back to the fact that the subject of Tyler's conversation had actually been Rosalind. She coughed and then took a quick sip of water. "I—I don't know how well she checked me out, but we did have a bit of a talk. She's a very nice lady. I liked her a lot."

"Yeah, she's a good person all right. Goes all out for her friends, and boy did she get on my case last night about you."

"Really?" Zelda's voice spiraled in surprise. "What on earth for?"

"She said I let Mathew get under my skin, and that my jealous reaction to your being at the party with him made you uncomfortable." He hesitated, his eyes scanning her face anxiously. "That's one of the reasons I came here tonight. I wanted to tell you I'm sorry if I anything I said or did upset you."

Zelda looked down at her plate to avoid his searching scrutiny. "It was an awkward situation for each of us, I realize that. And certainly Mathew made it worse." She frowned and pressed her lips together, wanting to explain, but uncertain as to how to go about it. "I'm not seeing Mathew, if that's what you think," she said finally.

Tyler shook his head. "I didn't actually believe that you were. But I freaked out anyway. Seeing you there with him was a downer for me. I was jealous—I have to admit it," he said grimly.

"There's no reason for you to be," she answered softly.

"You're so very important to me Zelda. That's my reason. I care more about you than anyone, ever. I want you to know that." His eyes met hers as he said this, and his gaze was as soft as a caress.

Suddenly, her heart seemed to pump relief through her veins and circulate serenity all though her body. He cared about her, she was important to him. Surely that meant there was a place for her in his life after all. She sighed, a gossamer smile crossing her lips. "That's a lovely reason, Tyler, and the best reason there could be for you and I to both just forget all about last night's party. In the scheme of things, it now seems totally unimportant."

"I couldn't agree with you more," he said, smiling his mercurial smile.

They both picked up their forks then and continued eating. A thread of understanding seemed to tie their two minds together and they finished their steak and potatoes in companionable silence.

Several minutes later, Zelda got up from the table to fix their chocolate sundaes for dessert. While she was doing this, Tyler removed their dinner plates, rinsed them, and placed them in the dishwasher.

"I think one of your girlfriends has certainly trained you well," Zelda told him, a teasing glint in her laughing eyes.

"Oh sure," he countered wryly. "There's a bevy of Lexington dolls who claim credit for my good habits and helpful ways."

"I don't doubt that for a minute." She quipped.

They both laughed and headed back to the table to have dessert. While they were eating the ice cream laden with gooey fudge sauce and sprinkled over with pecans, Zelda brought up the subject of her visit with Rosalind once again.

"Speaking of your good deeds and gentle-manly ways, Rosalind truly sings your praises. She finds you a good deal more charming than her nephew, she makes no bones about that."

Tyler passed Rosalind's complimentary words off with a shrug. "She was just put out with Mathew because of the way he acted last night. He's a good sort really. He's cool even, except when he thinks someone else is getting more attention than he is."

"Well, all I know is that Rosalind sure thinks the world of you. Sara did too. I imagine if Sara had lived, you and she would have married."

Tyler looked nonplussed hearing this. "Where on earth did you get an idea like that?"

Zelda shifted uneasily in her chair. "From what everyone says about her."

"And just what does everyone say?" He asked, a questioning frown now darkening his expression.

"That Sara idolized and adored you. That everyone who knew her loved her. And you loved her too—didn't you," she asked, her voice breaking slightly much to her dismay.

"Sure, I did. I loved Sara like my kid sister, because that was what she seemed to me. She was young, barely thirteen years old that first summer Nathan got me to work with her and Sweet Dream. Young and frail as a lily." He sighed and shook his head. "I remember looking at her and thinking, how can Nathan expect this thin little sparrow of a girl to be able to handle a horse, even one as gentle as the mare he'd bought her."

"But she did, and I know it was a remarkable achievement for her."

"You better believe it. Sara struggled like a flower toward heaven, never complaining and never giving up. Who wouldn't love a girl like that," he said, an intensity in his voice that hadn't been there before. "So, yes, I did love Sara, and our relationship was special, but it wasn't a romance and it never would have been."

Zelda felt her face growing warm with embarrassment. She was guilty of prying into Tyler's personal life. She had no doubts that Tyler knew that was exactly what she was doing. "I— I'm really sorry Tyler. I certainly shouldn't have asked such a personal question. Forgive me, please."

"That's okay. In fact I don't mind, because now you owe me one."

"Owe you one what?" she asked, frowning questioningly.

"One answer to a personal question I might want to ask you," he said smoothly, looking at her enigmatically.

"Fair enough—what's the question?"

His expressive face changed and became almost sober. "I don't have one quite yet. But I'm sure I will before long." He paused, and a slow smile began in his eyes and then moved cautiously to his lips. "You'll have to wait and see."

Tyler's words and manner intrigued her, but she resisted an impulse to push their discussion further. She looked at him with a sweet, musing look. "I'll do that, Tyler. I'll wait and see."

Chapter Eleven

Zelda's father returned the last day of July. The following week, he and Zelda got started cataloguing and pricing the contents of a large home in an older residential area of Lexington in preparation for the estate sale the end of August. It would be a major sale, similar in many ways to that of the Nathan Redmond's.

August came and brought skies as blue as cornflowers, yellow sunlight, and warm unmoving air. As the month progressed, the grass turned dry and brown and lay under trees from which branches leaves were beginning to fall. Zelda could smell faintly, through the vapors of the city, the meager earth under her feet as she walked across the lawn of this interesting estate.

It was located in an attractive area with well kept yards and gardens. All was quiet now with summer coming to an end. No frogs or crickets sang and only the far off hum of the city made a murmur like wind on water, and the drying grass made a warm sweet odor on the air.

As is usually the case with an Iverson sale, everything ran smoothly. The sale lasted four days and proved to be highly successful.

Zelda welcomed the slightly cooler days that came with September. Especially so because Tyler included her in the interesting happenings leading up to the September Yearling Sale at Keeneland. This meant she was spending a lot of time outdoors. The early fall days were clear with skies that had turned the translucent blue of butterfly wings. The golden light was like wine shining on tree leaves that had begun to mellow to rusty brown, magenta red, and mottled gold.

Tyler and Ernie had consigned two colts to be sold, an ebony coated yearling named Black Magic, and a sorrel Tyler called Lucky Penny because his dam was Pretty Penny and his sire a stakes winner called Lots of Luck. Both of these young horses had good lineage. Their family traits and race-track pedigrees were above average. Experts had researched each horse's family background as to what genetics have demonstrated through the years concerning the passing on of desired traits. Both came from family lines with acceptable performance records in stakes races.

All day long, the day proceeding the actual auction sale, Zelda watched and listened in amazement as the many professional buyers, trainers, pedigree analysts, and veterinarians approached Tyler and Ernie to inspect and evaluate Tyler's two yearlings.

"I had no idea selling thoroughbred horses was so involved. Why it's almost a scientific procedure the way they're examining your two horses," she told Tyler.

"They're thorough all right, but there's a lot of money involved, you know. The experienced buyer makes careful decisions about which horse's he's going to bid on. Once he's satisfied with the horse's pedigree, he then checks his conformation to be certain he's a well balanced horse."

She shook her head in puzzlement. "Conformation and being well balanced—what does that entail exactly?"

"Well, it means there needs to be symmetry and an alignment of muscles, bones, tendons and ligaments with one part flowing right into the next with no serious deviation to stop your eye as it travels over the horse's body. Look over there at Black Magic and you'll see what I'm talking about."

Zelda gazed toward where Ernie was now leading the black yearling on a walk for a team of three men to inspect him. "He's simply beautiful," Zelda said. "He looks perfectly aligned to me."

"Yeah, his conformation is good all right," Tyler said, a note of pride and satisfaction in his voice. "Now pay close attention to his walk. His stride should be free and easy at a walk. That buyer and trainer standing there and watching Black Magic, they want to see a good, solid, aggressive walk—not charging and not gawking around, just a good, brisk forward walk with a nice, long, free stride."

Just as Tyler said this, Ernie motioned to him. "Come over here, Tyler," he called.

Tyler took Zelda's hand. "You can come along, but stay a little in the background," he cautioned. "That's a buyer that bought a horse from me two years ago, and he has his trainer and his vet with him. I'm thinking he's getting serious about that old Black Magic." He gave her hand a squeeze as he said this, then with a sidelong wink he let go of her hand and strode rapidly over to join the men.

"Mighty fine looking yearling you've got here, Wakefield," the oldest of the three men, who

Zelda thought obviously was the buyer Tyler knew, addressed Tyler with a cordial smile followed by a friendly clap on the shoulder. "Good eye and strong, straight neck on this horse. I like that. Not a bad v-shaped neck but a bit on the narrow side perhaps. What do you think about that, Carl?" he asked, directing his attention to one of the other men with him.

"It's been my experience that if I have to cope with one or the other, I prefer a horse that is narrow in the chest to one that is too wide."

"Why is that?"

"The wide chested horse simply isn't going to have proper balance and alignment, and as a result isn't going to have freedom of movement or proper distribution of concussion."

"I can see how that makes sense," the buyer agreed. And Carl, since you're the guy who's going be training whichever horse we buy, I sure want your input." He nodded his head, crossed his arms across his chest and turned back to Tyler. "Now I'd like to look over your other yearling, Wakefield," he said.

"Fine. I'll walk Lucky Penny out for you." Tyler said.

Aware of how important it was for both Tyler and Ernie to give their full attention to showing the colts, and since she'd already been here at Keeneland with Tyler most of the day, Zelda quickly decided that it was time for her to excuse herself and get out of the way. "I'm going to leave now, Tyler," she hurried to say. "Catch you later."

He gave her an agreeing nod, then hurried off to fetch Lucky Penny.

The following day was the sales session which would include the two yearlings consigned by Wakefield Farm. Tyler had requested four seats in the sales pavilion for Martha and Ernie and Zelda and him. Priority in seating is given to persons who have filed an authorization to bid form. Since Tyler was a consignor, not a bidder, their seats were about three quarters of the way back from the sales ring.

The sale was to begin at ten o'clock that morning. Martha and Zelda were in their seats ahead of the fellows. Ernie and Tyler joined them about the same time as the auctioneer got to his stand, which was in the middle of the sales ring.

Once the sale began, things happened in a rapid-fire fashion. Each colt or filly came into the sales ring in beautiful condition with its coat gleaming and its mane and tail all neatly combed. Zelda quickly discovered that the average yearling was actually in the sales ring only a minute and a half to two minutes. Tyler had explained a little about the bidding process to her before hand, but being there and actually seeing it in action proved more exciting than she ever could have imagined. Of course auctioneers are paid to sell horses and they are very skillful at it. Zelda quickly discovered that this Keeneland auctioneer would do everything he could to turn the bidding into a fast-paced competition. She watched and listened in fascination. It took her until perhaps a dozen horses were sold before she caught on to the auctioneer's rhythm. Then she realized that once all of the frenzied bidding is over and the hype ended, the auctioneer slows his chant, looks around and there is always that final pause before his hammer falls and he says, "Sold".

This year the September Yearling Sale was to cover two days with approximately three hundred and eighty five horses consigned for sale on each day. It was midway into the day's sales before the first of Tyler's colts, the sorrel brown Lucky Penny came to the sales ring. Zelda glanced at Tyler, her excitement making her feel a little breathless. Tyler looked strained. Watching him rub the heels of both hands into his eyes, Zelda began to see how much this sale meant to him.

A moment later the auctioneer began his chant. As is normally done, the auctioneer starts the horse at a higher figure than anyone is willing to bid. Tyler had explained this to her, but even so, Zelda's eyes widened in surprise as he started out with a higher figure than she'd heard before in this sale. In a matter of seconds he lowered the starting price to a realistic level and the stir of activity was immediate. As the bidding escalated rapidly a look of exhilaration wiped the tiredness from Tyler's earlier expression. When the final bid came, Tyler shot Ernie a triumphant look.

The excited Ernie gave Tyler a conspiratorial wink. "Way to go, man!" he whooped.

Tyler grinned. "We're getting there, Ernie. We're really getting there."

Less than an hour later, Black Magic was in the sales ring. The auctioneer again started his chant and in short order the first bid was made by the man Tyler had sold a horse to once before. "That's Lee Gillette," he told Zelda, pointing him out to her. "He's the fellow you saw yesterday when he and his trainer were at the barn with their vet examining our colts."

While Tyler was saying this, there were bids popping up all around the sales area. This continued for several seconds, and then it became a bidding contest between Lee Gillette and a trainer who was acting as an agent for his employer. These two bidders competed for perhaps thirty or forty seconds, raising each other with increasing amounts. Finally they reached a price where one bidder dropped out. The auctioneer paused for a brief moment, giving him time to come back to top the last bid, before he dropped his hammer, pointed his finger at the final bidder and called, "Sold".

It all happened fast, and Zelda looked to Tyler in confusion. "Which man bought him?" she asked, shaking her head. "I couldn't follow everything."

"Lee Gillette," Tyler said, a ring of satisfaction in his elated voice. "And he uses one of the best trainers in the business, Carl Nafzger. It wouldn't surprise me one bit if Carl makes a high stakes winner of our Black Magic."

"Boy, that was some bidding contest," Ernie said, coming over to clap Tyler's shoulder. "I'd say this was a great day for Wakefield Farm."

"Yeah, those two yearlings did us proud." Tyler's face was beaming. "We did it right all the way, ol' friend."

Ernie's face split in a wide grin. "That we did," Ernie agreed wholeheartedly.

Martha and Zelda were standing next to the fellows listening to them carry one. "Before these two both break an arm patting themselves on the back, lets see if we can't drag them out of here," Martha said, laughing and giving Zelda a nudge with her elbow. "You take charge of

Tyler and I'll try to budge this gabby husband of mine."

"We can take a hint, can't we, Ernie," Tyler said, bestowing a good natured smile on Martha and looping his arm through Zelda's. "So let's all go celebrate. It's my treat, and the four of us are going to Vinelli's and eat great pasta and drink red wine. How does that grab everybody?"

"Sounds super to me," Zelda said.

"Thanks, Tyler. I sure wish we could, but our son is driving over from Louisville with a bunch of dwarf shrubs I've been wanting. Ernie and I have to be home to help him plant them." Martha explained.

Ernie shrugged. "Yeah, Martha has to supervise everything that gets put in the ground at our place down to the last blade of grass. We all know that," Ernie added with a teasing grin. "We'll have to take a rain check, but you two have a high time and celebrate Wakefield Farm's day of wealth and glory."

With this, the four of them left the sales pavilion, then parted to go to their cars. Tyler's mood was jubilant, and holding fast to Zelda's hand the two of them covered the distance to his car almost at a run.

"I haven't had a chance to tell you how happy I am for you," Zelda told him, her voice breathless now from keeping up with him. "I know you're feeling good with the way the sale went."

"Good isn't even half of it. I feel stupendous," he cried, giving her a bear hug as he lifted her feet off the ground and spun her around in a dizzy circle. "And you know, the best part was having you right there beside me. You bring me luck, Zelda. Promise me you'll always be my good-luck charm."

"I can't promise you anything while you're squeezing the breath out of me and making me tipsy," she gasped, laughing.

"Oh, I'm sorry," he said, letting her down so her feet could just touch the ground. "I can't help getting carried away at times, expecially when I'm with you." He eased his hold around her, but still kept his arms around her. "I think you should know by now that you're not only my good-luck charm. You're everything to me, Zelda—everything I want and love."

Tyler was looking deep into her eyes as he said this. As they both gazed at each other for a long moment, Zelda remembered that it was said lovers see each other's reflection in their eyes. For an instant she caught her own image in the two circles of Tyler's dark eyes. Then she saw nothing more, for he had drawn her close. She trembled, and leaning against him, gave him all her weight, so that, half-lifted, her feet barely grazed the ground and she was held to him by arms and lips.

Chapter Twelve

"You are everything I want and love." Tyler had said that to her, and now his words kept playing through her head like a romantic song. In fact, she found herself humming snatches of tunes, singing words and phrases that surfaced in her mind, even experimenting with various ways to make them rhyme.

> You are to me everything,
> Summer, fall, winter, spring.
> The sun, moon, and stars above,
> You are everything I love.

As she sang she smiled to herself because she was so happy. She laughed at herself a little too, because she was being slightly foolish, but she didn't care. She was in love.

With the coming of autumn, Zelda was exceedingly busy with her work. Iverson's had two estate sales to handle during the month of October and one of these was in Louisville. So for several weeks she and her father traveled the fifty odd miles to Louisville each day to do the cataloguing and pricing, and also to arrange for the announcements of the sale to be published in the city newspaper.

During this time, she saw relatively little of Tyler. That is why she was anxious for the upcoming weekend to get here, because she and Tyler would have all day together. It was the weekend of the annual Pumpkin Fest. It was the fun event of every fall, and featured hayrides, pumpkin-carving demonstrations, and a craft display and sale that was second to none.

Saturday was a bright October day complete with a blue ribbon sky, and fringed with golden sun. Zelda's first priority was to scout through the large array of various size pumpkins. It took her about twenty minutes before she decided on a fat, deep orange one that she planned to set in one corner of her front porch surrounded by some tri-colored corn as a decoration for harvest season and Halloween. Having made her purchase, she encouraged Tyler to consider doing the same.

"You have that attractive front porch that stretches all across the front of your house. An arrangement of corn and two or three different size pumpkins by your front door would look inviting."

"I suppose that would give my house that woman's touch that Martha claims it needs." He smiled wryly. "Don't you think?"

"Could be," she said, the corners of her mouth lifting into a knowing smile. "Certainly would add a nice autumn touch, at any rate. And I'm sure Martha will notice and make a pertinent comment."

"There's no doubt about that." He laughed and then reached down and picked out three pumpkins, one large, one medium size and a third small, the size of a cantaloupe.

With the help of a wheelbarrow, provided by the pumpkin farmer, Tyler and Zelda loaded their pumpkins and a generous quantity of the three-colored corn in Tyler's van. They then went back to watch the pumpkin-carving demonstration.

After that, they stolled leisurely around the open-air market, taking in all the bake-sale and home-canned items and doing some shopping. Zelda bought a jar of homemade apple butter to take home to her dad, and a jar each of mint jelly, strawberry jam, and peach preserves. Tyler opted for a box of fudge and a package of luscious looking pecan pralines.

"I didn't realize you had such a sweet tooth," Zelda said, eyeing the rich candies warily.

"Oh, mine is only marginal. I'm really going to share most of this with Ernie."

"Yeah, I bet," she mocked him, laughing.

"Okay, okay," Tyler muttered. Let's move away from all these sweet temptations and go look at the arts and crafts stuff. I've got greater sales resistance when it's something I can't eat."

A craft fair in Kentucky is not complete without a sizeable display of horse related items. This one today turned out to be a horse-shopping haven. They had horse earrings and charm bracelets, horsey clothing such as tee shirts, caps, scarves and ties, greeting cards, note paper, whatnots, coasters, boxes, figurines, and even lamps and paintings.

Zelda was immediately attracted to the great designs on the silk scarves. She took a lot of time examining a number of them, searching for the right color combination to go with her camel colored cashmere jacket. While she was doing this, Tyler wandered away to look at other items besides clothing.

Zelda finally selected the scarf she wanted,

and once she'd paid for it, she glanced around to locate Tyler. When she caught sight of him, it was obvious that he'd bought something too, for he was carrying a small plastic sack that he hadn't had before.

"I bought a sensational silk scarf," she said when she caught up to him. "What did you buy?"

"Just a little something that caught my eye."

"Let me see it."

Tyler shook his head. "Not now. Anyway it's all wrapped up in some of that bubble plastic so it won't get damaged."

"Oh, is it breakable?" she asked, screwing her face up like a curious rabbit.

"Yeah. That's why I want to handle it carefully."

"Then just tell me what it is? Does it have something to do with horses?"

"You're sure inquisitive, you know that? I'll let you see it later. Besides, it's kind of a surprise." He had lowered his voice, being purposefully mysterious, at least that's what Zelda thought.

"I love surprises," she said softly, her eyes narrowing thoughtfully. "And you've got me very intrigued about this one."

Tyler shook his head at her. "Give it up, Zelda. No amount of sweet talk will make me change my mind. You have to wait until we go to dinner."

"She made a face and shrugged her shoulders. "Okay." She gave him a resigned smile. "Then lets go have a look at the needlecraft and hand-loomed things and then leave for dinner."

Joe Vinelli was back in Lexington for the entire month of October. He was engaged to ride in a lot of the races that were to be held throughout October at Keeneland Racetrack. In fact, he'd ridden in three races there this afternoon. He'd invited Tyler and Zelda to join him for dinner at Villa Vinelli at six that evening. He'd specified the early hour because when he was in town on weekends, he took over for his father at the front, greeting customers from eight o'clock until closing. On Friday and Saturday nights, the place was usually crowded with exuberant groups of young couples. Joe's fame as a jockey made him a familiar and popular figure with this thirty-something crowd.

The streets outside Villa Vinelli were blue and misty with dusk as Tyler and Zelda drove into the parking area. Evening sounds were in the air and as they entered the restaurant, there was the sound of recorded dinner music and the appetizing odors of spicy Italian food and aromatic wine.

Joe had a table all arranged for the three of them, and as soon as they were seated, Tyler began questioning him about today's races.

"Tell me who you were riding for and how well your horses did?"

"It was an interesting day, not spectacular, but with a number of rewarding moments." Joe said, his round eyes shining like pieces of mica.

Zelda smiled at him. "Sounds like you had a win, place or, show."

"Well I came in fifth in the first race, but third in the second one. Then in the final race my horse came down to the wire head to head with today's favorite. The favorite won by a nose, but it was a great run and second place held sweet rewards." Joe turned to Tyler. "You'll be interested to know who owns Night Song, the two-year-old bay I rode."

"Who?" Tyler asked, his eyebrows raised inquiringly.

"Averill Javerman, no less." Joe told him.

"Who's he?" Zelda asked.

Joe looked at her in surprise, as if he couldn't believe she didn't know. "He's just someone that horse breeders are glad to know. He's wealthy and more than willing to pay in six figures for a thoroughbred yearling that he takes a fancy to. And he wants me to bring him out to Wakefield

Farm to take a look around. How about that great news?"

Tyler frowned. "Did you tell him something about Dream Maker. Is that why he's coming?"

"Yeah, I mentioned a few things," Joe said, a smug expression marking his jovial face. "And you know, don't you Tyler, that if he should buy that colt of yours, he'd pay you even more than you'd get at next July's selected yearling sale."

"That's probably true all right. But you see, I'm not selling Dream Maker." He shook his head. "Not at any price."

"Oh, thank goodness!" Zelda interjected, heaving a sigh of relief. "You had me scared to death there for a minute, Tyler."

Tyler reached over and laid his hand on her arm. "Don't you worry," he said gently, his mouth curving into an unconscious smile. "There are three of us concerned with Dream Maker, you, me, and Ernie. We three will be together on all decisions regarding our horse." The warm pressure of his hand on her arm emphasized his words.

Joe shrugged and gave a good natured chuckle. "Well, I was trying to make the big bucks for you and I goofed."

"I appreciate that, Joe. I'd sure like to get Javerman interested in some other colt of mine, but I want to try my luck with Dream Maker. I've got a special feeling about this horse and I'm going to follow the advice my dad gave me. He said, 'Saddle a dream, then just ride to win,' and that's what I intend to do."

Joe had arranged their meal ahead, selecting some of the Villa Vinelli's special dishes. Promptly now, Marya, the young, pretty Italian waitress appeared with a leafy green salad tossed with Italian dressing and Parmesan cheese and a basket of crusty Italian bread. She then filled their round bowled glasses with red wine, left their table for a few minutes, then returned with their dinner of Lasagne Verde with meat sauce and cheese. It was a house specialty and the delicate green color of the pasta resulted from the finely chopped spinach that had been kneaded into it. As Joe so often said, "the way my mother makes Lasagne Verde is fabulous— it's to die for." Zelda was quick to agree that he was so right.

With their conversation now turned to food, Joe said, "I've worked up a hearty appetite after riding in three races. I can eat everything in sight."

"I can second that," Tyler agreed. "Zelda kept me on the move all afternoon. She didn't let me miss a thing at the Pumpkin Fest. More than that, you should see all the pumpkins and corn stalks we bought that I had to handle, move back out, and load in the car."

"With the help of a wheelbarrow," Zelda hastened to add. "And the distance was only about two hundred yards. Hardly a Herculean feat," she chided him, laughing.

"Whatever, but at any rate I'm plenty hungry," he countered, attacking his lasagne with gusto.

Joe was never one to be quiet for long, so he kept the conversation going as they enjoyed their dinner. Joe's dad served their desserts himself, frozen Zabaglione in sherbet glasses accompanied by lady fingers. He stayed and talked with them for just a few minutes, but he couldn't stay long as the seven-thirty crowd was rapidly filling the few vacated tables.

The Zabaglione tasted lucious and creamy. It was full of crystallized fruits, with lots of cherries and strawberries. It was not only pretty to look at, but delicious to taste.

By this time, Joe evidently felt he was needed to help out in the restaurant. "Stay and have another cup of coffee," he urged them, as they thanked him for dinner. Then he hurried off.

As soon as they were alone, Tyler set down his coffee cup and gave his full attention to Zelda. "I didn't want to bring it up with Joe here, but do you still want to see the little thing I bought this afternoon?" he asked, his face creasing into a sudden smile.

Zelda's eyes lit up at this. "Absolutely! Are you going to let me see it now?" Her voice held a note of pleased expectancy.

"I'm a man of my word, and I said you could look at it when we had dinner."

"But you left it in the car didn't you."

He shook his head. "No, I smuggled it in."

"Well, where is it?" She prodded him, looking all around and even under the table. "I don't see a sign of a sack anywhere.

"It's in the empty chair under my jacket and your sweater." He stood up quickly as he said this, going around the table to the chair he'd indicated and slipping his hand in under their wraps. "Voila!" he exclaimed as he produced the small package in the manner of a magician pulling a rabbit out of a hat. "A little present for you, darling," he said, giving her a smile that was as intimate as a kiss.

Zelda looked at him, a small smile of enchantment touching her lips. "You mean it's for me— I thought you'd gotten some horse-theme thing for yourself."

"You thought wrong. I got a little *what's it* that is definitely not a man's thing."

Zelda had already started undoing the bubble plastic that enclosed a small tissue paper wrapped object. Now she quickly romoved the tissue, excitement causing her fingers to tremble. "Oh, Tyler, how perfectly lovely," she exclaimed, discovering a small, round porcelain china box with an exquisitely hand-painted picture on the lid of a golden brown horse with her foal at her side. "This looks exactly like Sweet Dream and Dream Maker that first day I saw them. I love it, Tyler," she exclaimed happily. "Thank you," she added with a blissful sigh.

Tyler smiled, obviously he was gratified by her reaction. "Look, I think we probably should get out of here. I'm sure there are people waiting for a table."

Zelda nodded and stood up. Tyler placed her sweater around her shoulders. "Besides, I want to get you all to myself where we can talk about something important," he whispered, leaning his face close to hers so she felt his soft breath fan her cheek.

She felt a ripple of excitement at his words. "I'm all for that," she said, with a slow secret smile. "I have something nice to tell you too. I've just been waiting for the right time, and something that was said earlier tonight makes me feel I should tell you now."

Tyler eyebrows rose inquiringly. "Okay, I'm all for that." He grabbed her hand, and his smile echoed hers as they walked out of Villa Vinelli together.

Chapter Thirteen

Outside, there was a funny old lopsided moon shining through some tattered scraps of clouds. As they drove rather leisurely along one of the thoroughfares that led out to the residential area where she lived, Zelda rolled down the car window and let the pleasant night air blow in. It felt velvety soft touching her face.

"I have the nicest surprise for you, Tyler." Her voice had a low silvery tone. "I know I'm probably telling you about it way too soon, but I think you'll be so pleased to know it, I'm going to tell you now anyway."

"I do hope so. The way you're going on I was afraid you'd talk yourself out of telling me anything at all."

She wrinkled her nose at him. "This is special, and I need to give you the background on it. So don't try to be funny. Just pay attention."

He wiped the jesting smile from his face. "Okay. I will listen carefully, solemnly, and without any interruptions."

She smiled. "Good, you can comment, though, if something isn't clear." She hesitated a moment, deciding just where was the best place to start. "You remember tonight when Joe was talking about the prospect of your selling Dream Maker," she said finally.

Tyler nodded. "He surprised me. I thought he knew I had no intention of letting Dream Maker leave Wakefield Farm."

"I think he figured if you were offered a really impressive price, you'd sell. That's why I was so relieved when you said what you did—about you, me, and Ernie sharing in the hopes and dreams concerning Dream Maker."

Tyler smiled. "Yeah, we're all together in this. We're two guys, a girl, and horse."

"Actually Tyler, there's one other person concerned in this. Someone who counted on playing a special and important part."

He took his eyes off the road long enough to study her with a speculative look. "Sounds interesting and rather mysterious, and I don't have a clue as to the person you're talking about. So, who in the world is it?"

"Before I tell you, we need to go back a bit, so you have the whole picture."

"Honestly, Zelda," he interrupted her, a note of exasperation in his voice. "Why do women have to make a production of telling a fellow something as simple as a person's name."

"Because you need the background to get the full impact of my story," she told him, wrapping her words in a good natured smile. "Besides, what I'm going to tell you has a super nice surprise ending. Isn't that worth indulging me in a couple of minutes of preliminary build-up?"

"Yes it is. I apologize for my impatient male attitude." He was teasing her affectionately, and he grimaced now in good humor.

"Okay, bear with me for just a second. You recall the money that you found among the letters and pictures in that box of Nathan's you bought at the sale."

"Yeah, sure I do. Why that money gave me a good excuse to see you again. When I returned the money to you we had our first date, remember? That was a big break for me. You might not have gone out with me otherwise."

She smiled knowingly. "Yes, I would have. All you needed to do was ask me. But let me get back to the money. As you suspected, it was

Rosalind who had sent it to Nathan to be used for a specific purpose."

"But Nathan hadn't done anything with it."

"No, of course he hadn't. Because the right time hadn't come for him to do it," Zelda said with an emphatic bob of her head. Furthermore, it wasn't Rosalind's money in the first place."

Tyler frowned and shook his head in bewilderment. "For pete sake, whose was it then?"

"It was Sara's." Zelda stressed each word dramatically.

Tyler looked totally confused. "Sara's! How could that be?"

"It was money she'd saved up out of her allowance, probably. She had put it aside to be used for a special project that was of great importance to her. And the reason it meant so much to her is because it was something she could do for you after all you'd done for her."

They had reached Zelda's house by now, and Tyler pulled into the driveway and turned off the ignition before he turned and faced her. "This is mind boggling to me. I can tell you that," he said. There was an oddly touching expression on Tyler's face, rather nostalgic and somewhat melancholy.

"I can well imagine that it is, Tyler. But wait until I tell what it is she's giving you. You're going to be amazed and so pleased," she said, reaching over to touch his hand which still rested on the steering wheel. "Sara saved her money so she could be the one to buy your Wakefield silks for you. So, you see there really are four of us concerned in what happens with Dream Maker. We're two guys, *two* girls, and a horse," she said softly.

"Wakefield Farm silks—well what do you know," he said, a tremor of emotion in his husky voice. "It is so like Sara to want to do this. She's a special girl, our Sara." His voice was low, almost a murmur. Then he exhaled a long sigh of contentment.

"I guess you've figured out that Rosalind told me all about this when she was here. She gave me the money and now all you have to do is tell me the design, and the two colors you want, and I'll take care of the rest."

He rubbed his chin with his thumb and forefinger, a thoughtful look creasing his forehead. "I really haven't thought too much about our racing silks as yet, and I'll definitely need your help on the colors." He paused, his frown growing deeper. "I can tell you two colors I don't want though."

"What are they?"

"Red or purple." He bobbed his head decisively. There's a lot of red out there already, and as for purple, I know a prominent owner-trainer who has purple and white silks. I don't like that color too much anyway."

"I think you need a color that just goes with Wakefield Farm. One that is a natural for it like its green roofs and green grass." She smiled tentatively. "What do you think?"

Tyler rewarded her with a larger smile of his own. "Without a doubt, green is the perfect choice for the main color. I can visualize it now—a clear, bright green that matches our roofs, our grassy pastures, and the color of the winner's money," he said with a wink and a chuckle. "Now let's talk about the color we want to go with green."

Zelda tapped her lips thoughtfully. After a moment she said, "I think green and white would be okay. That's kind of classic, I feel. What do you think?"

He shrugged. "White's all right," he said, sounding disinterested. "It just doesn't send me very far though." He paused for a minute, then looked at Zelda, smiled, and nodded his head. "You know what just occurred to me is a color that Sara liked. That is a nice, bright, cheerful yellow."

"That's great," she agreed enthusiastically. Green and yellow is super."

Tyler beamed. "Yeah, it is. And Sara would like the green and yellow combination. She'd say—'whoa man—that's cool.' " His pleased expression broadened into a grin. "It's settled than. Wakefield Farm will have green and yellow racing silks. A green jockey cap, and a shirt with broad green and yellow stripes going around rather than up and down. And to add a touch of class and make it distinctive, let's have one sleeve of the shirt yellow and the other green."

Zelda listened to Tyler description with a slightly amused expression on her face. "You know, Tyler, it sounds to me like you've given more thought to these silks than you realized."

He gave her a sheepish grin. "Yeah, I suppose I have," he chuckled.

Zelda reached for the door handle on her side. "Now that we've settled this quickly and easily, how about going into my house with me?" She didn't wait for him to agree, she just slid out of her seat and headed off.

Tyler wasted no time in following suit however. He quickly caught up with her, looped his arm through hers, and synchronized his steps to hers as they marched to her front porch.

As soon as Zelda unlocked the door, they went in together, walking through the softly lit entry hall to the family room. "Oh good," Zelda muttered, seeing that her father had left two lamps on, one by his favorite camel brown leather lounge chair and the other on the table at the end of the wheat colored, cushioned sofa. "Dad knows I don't like to come home to a dark house. The rule is to leave the entry light on, but bless his heart, he went all out with these two lights on in here. It even looks like the mini-lamp by the telephone in the kitchen is on. I'll go check to see if Dad left it so I'd check the messages. I'll tell you what, while I do that, you put on some music and get settled in a comfortable spot."

"Better still—I'll go bring in your pumpkin and stuff from the back of the van. I was about to forget to do that."

"Me too—I'll come with you right now and help."

Tyler shook his head. "No you won't," he said emphatically. "You do what you need to. I'll do it alone. I'm not going to be razzed by you again about needing a wheelbarrow or any assistance from you. See, I've got two strong hands." He stuck them out directly in her face. "I can take care of everything just fine."

Zelda's mouth twitched with amusement. "I don't doubt it for a minute. Just put the pumpkin on the porch and stack the corn there too. I'll arrange it the way I want to in the morning. But don't forget my sack with the jars of jelly and the other package that has my designer scarf. Bring those things inside." She angled her head at him and gave him her most ingratiatory smile. "And I thank you very much, Tyler. I don't know what I'd ever do without you."

"If I have my way about it, you'll never have to," he said, his gaze riveted on her face and his eyes searched hers.

Suddenly, beneath their light banter, Zelda was filled with feelings of suppressed excitement and tingles of anticipation. "Don't be too long," she said softly.

He touched her face and his hand was gentle on her cheek as he drifted a finger caressingly to touch her lips. "Three minutes—four at the outside." He dropped his hand and took a step in the direction of the front door.

At the same time, she turned and walked to the kitchen, still experiencing a little rush of warmth to her face where Tyler's hand had touched her cheek and his finger brushed her lips.

By the time Tyler came back in, Zelda had music playing softly and was at this moment placing a carafe and two ice filled glasses on the low table in front of the sofa. "I don't know about you, Tyler, but after that great Italian pasta and cheese we've eaten, I'm thirsty. I thought you might like to have some plain old ice water too." She filled one of the glasses as she spoke. Then when Tyler gave an agreeing nod, she filled the second glass, handing it to him as soon as he joined her on the sofa.

"You know, I've been thinking about all that was said at dinner tonight. It was interesting to me, and I've been thinking about some of the things ever since."

"What thing in particular?" he asked, relaxing his back against the comfortable sofa cushions and stretching his long legs leisurely before him.

"Most importantly, I was taken with your father's advice to you about saddling your dream and going for it. I liked the way you said he put it—reminded me in a way of the motto that's been handed down in our family for at least a century."

"What is it?"

"Hitch your wagon to a star. 'Course that's of much older vintage than yours." She gave a nostalgic sigh. "When I was a little girl the idea of my wagon climbing up to the stars made a lasting impression on me. Just like your dad's encouraging words have stayed with you. Kind of a nice legacy for each of us, isn't it?"

"You bet it is," he said firmly.

They looked at each other then, exchanging an understanding sort of smile. There was silence between them for a moment. Then Zelda broke their reverie saying, "Tyler, tell me about your father. I'd like to know what he was like. You know why?"

"I guess, because like most females, you're by nature the inquisitive sex. Plus I've been around you enough to know you are a great one for question and answer games." There was a trace of laughter in his voice.

"I shouldn't even tell you why after that," she said, wrinkling her nose at him. "But seeing as how I'm *by nature* also a good sport, I'll overlook your remarks and tell you why anyway. You see I have an idea that you're a lot like your dad. When you're not trying to be funny, that is." She eyed him thoughtfully for a second, then added, "I'm even thinking that your father was a man who was all heart, and that since you told me that's the kind of man you are, then I'm guessing you got that quality from him. Am I right?"

Tyler's face sobered at this and his earnest eyes looked at her intently. "I hope I'm like him. I've tried to be. I doubt, however, that I could ever be as courageous or altruistic as he was."

"Why do you say that?"

"Well, for one thing, the kind of work he did put him at risk. He was with the State Highway Patrol. He'd been with them for six years when he and Mother got married. Mother was never too happy about his job. She worried about him being out on the highway day and night."

"I can see why that would make her anxious."

"But it was work that suited Dad, and he did well. He also had interesting and exciting tales to tell about different things that happened. As a kid I loved those first hand accounts. His stories were as good or better than the good-guy-bad-guy shows on television." Tyler chuckled to himself as he told her this. Zelda sensed these were especially happy recollections for him. "By the time I was about fifteen, however," Tyler continued, "Dad had been with the Highway Patrol over twenty years. So to please my mother, he left the State Police and went with a security service company. It was at this time that Nathan hired him to handle security at the bank."

"I didn't realize that your father worked at the bank. I guess it was through Nathan's connection with your dad, then, that led to his interest in your family and you in particular. You call him your benefactor, so I suppose that's how it came about. Right?"

Tyler stirred uneasily, shifting his position on the sofa. "It's sort of an involved story in some ways," he said, a disturbed look replacing his earlier relaxed expression. "But the reason Nathan did so much for us was because my father saved his life during a hold up at the bank."

"Good grief, Tyler! What happened?"

Tyler's brows drew together in an agonized expression. "I wasn't there, of course, and the report we were given at the time was that the robber freaked out and threatened Nathan, turning his gun on him. My dad jumped in front of Nathan to shield him and the bullet struck Dad and killed him instead."

Zelda sucked in her breath, her face contorted with shock. "Oh Tyler, what a terrible tragedy. I had no idea your father died like that. Such a horrible thing to happen, so heartbreaking for your mother and you. I—I'm so—so very sorry," she stammered, her voice fragile and shaking. She sighed, looking down at her hands that she had clenched together and pressed in her lap. She shook her head sadly and then spoke again. "I can understand now why Nathan wanted to do everything he possibly could for you and your mother. Even so, his endless gratitude could never equal your father's heroism." She shook her head again, then lifted her eyes and looked at Tyler, her lips pursed thoughtfully. "I'm now beginning to understand something Rosalind said to me that day she came to buy the paperweight."

Tyler quirked his eyebrow questioningly. "What did she say?"

"Well, it was rather odd actually. We'd been talking about Sara, and you're helping her, and about Nathan's interest and supportive encouragement to you. I said something about how appreciative you were, and that you were indebted to Nathan for being such a benefactor. When I said that, Rosalind immediately said that her father was more deeply indebted to you and your family than anyone would probably understand. She was sort of obscure about it, so it sounded like some kind of mystery to me. I asked her what she meant exactly. Then she started to leave and just said that it was a complex thing and that you should be the one to tell me, or words to that effect." She paused, crossing her arms, and appearing more relaxed. "I now see what she meant since you've told me about your father saving Nathan's life."

"Actually, there's a little more to it than that." He frowned and his face was grim as he continued. "What Rosalind is referring to are the circumstances that led up to my dad getting killed. It was something concerning Nathan, something that he and my father were the only ones to know about, so, Nathan never told anyone. He kept it a secret for years, in fact, he probably never would have told me or his family about it if Barton and Mathew hadn't been outraged and raised a ruckus about my getting a loan from the bank to buy the horse farm. Barton tried to block the deal, saying that I had railroaded Nathan to do all that he did for me just because my father had saved Nathan's life. Barton kept saying that what my dad did was just part of his job, and though it was unfortunate that he was killed in the line of duty, Nathan was not responsible. Furthermore, Barton said he would find a way to prevent me from getting a loan from their bank, then or ever."

"Wow! That had to have been an ugly scene."

"Yeah, it was bad all right. And what followed was so hard for Nathan to tell and for me to hear."

"Then this is the part that Rosalind was talking about, isn't it?"

"Yes, it's Nathan's story of exactly how the bank robbery went down. When he told me about it, he did it quietly and simply, and as long as I live I will never forget the pain and regret that I heard in his voice." Tyler paused and rubbed his hand back and forth across his forehead as if recollecting the exact details. "It was the middle of the morning on a November day, a week or so before Thanksgiving. Nathan said that besides the bank employees there were five customers in the bank. Then a sixth person entered the bank. He was a white male, approximately thirty years of age, about five-foot-ten and weighing one hundred-sixty to seventy pounds. He was wearing dark gray cotton work pants, a black zip front jacket, and a black base-ball cap pulled down low so the bill would shield his eyes. He carried a canvas gym type bag in his left hand, and when he got to the center of the bank, close to one of the teller counters, he drew a gun from inside his jacket with his right hand. Brandishing the gun menacingly, he ordered everyone to lie down on the floor with their head facing the wall. 'Don't move a muscle and nobody gets hurt,' he told them in a raspy voice that had an excitable edge to it."

"Nathan said that at the time, he and my dad were standing beside one of the loan officer's desks. Dad quickly pulled Nathan down on the floor beside him. Dad whispered to him that the robber could be high on something, and so no matter what happened, Nathan was not to so much as move a finger. 'Keep your face hidden,' Dad cautioned him. 'It's better if he doesn't recognize you as an officer of the bank. Above all, we don't want anyone to get hurt. So lie still and don't utter a word. I'll tell you when it's okay for any of us to move.' "

"Nathan explained that with his face down he couldn't see anything that was going on, of course. But he could hear the hold-up fellow moving around, obviously grabbing up all the money from the tellers' stalls. He said it was probably only six or seven minutes, but it seemed much longer. Then he heard some foot-steps walk fairly close to where he and Dad were lying. He judged the robber was moving toward the entrance to make his get away.'"

"At that point Nathan said the fellow ordered everybody to begin counting to two hundred. He warned them that he'd shoot anyone who moved or stopped counting. When my dad started count-ing in a clear, calm voice, Nathan said he fol-lowed right along. 'I counted to thirty,' he told me. 'Then I don't know why in the world I did it, but I lifted my head, figuring the robber had gone. But of course, he hadn't.'"

" 'Say ol' man, you don't listen too good, and that's too bad 'cause now you're dead, this guy yells at me. Then he aimed his gun at me, and in that split second your dad rolled over and cov-ered my body with his just as the shot was fired.' That was what actually happened Nathan said."

A look of shocked sadness marked Zelda's face. She stared at Tyler, too stunned to speak.

Tyler heaved a rugged sigh. "When Nathan finished telling his story, he turned to me with tears in his eyes. 'If it hadn't been for me, your father would be alive today,' he said. 'I was re-sponsible for what happened and I'll regret it for as long as I live. I can't take his place, but I will be there for you, always, just as he would have been.' It was a singular moment between Nathan and me. One we never spoke about again."

Zelda's eyes welled with sympathetic tears. "It's all so tragic, so infinitely sad. I almost wish Nathan had never told you."

Tyler nodded his head slowly. "Sometimes, I've wished that too," he said.

Chapter Fourteen

It wasn't until after lunch the following day that Zelda had time to decorate her front porch with fall foliage, the pumpkin, and the tri-colored corn she'd gotten at the pumpkin fest. By the time she'd arranged everything in an attractive and most effective manner, she found she had scads of the corn left over. Obviously Tyler had not divided it between them and consequently must not have taken any to the farm for himself.

Chiding herself because she had more or less forced Tyler to buy the pumpkins and corn to decorate his porch in the first place, she certainly needed to make sure that everything got used properly. Like Martha pointed out, Tyler's house could use a woman's touch, and since the porch project had been her idea she would help Tyler carry it out. With this thought in mind, she went inside to call and tell him about the corn.

She unzipped the denim jacket she'd worn to work outside in the brisk October air just as her phone began to ring. Tossing the jacket over the back of a dining room chair, she dashed into the kitchen, grabbing up the receiver on the fourth ring, a split second before the answering machine would have clicked on.

"Hello," she muttered hastily.

"Hello, yourself," Tyler's mellow voice had the sound of a smile in it. "I hope I didn't pull you away from something important."

"No, no," she was quick to assure him. "The fact is that you and I must be on the same wave length, because I'd just come into the house to call you."

"Hey, I like hearing that. What's on your mind?"

"A big supply of corn."

"In the can or on the cob," he quipped.

"Unhusked complete with stalks," she countered, half laughing.

Tyler's laughter floated up from his throat. "You're talking about that funny colored stuff we bought yesterday, I guess."

"You guessed right. And I suppose you realize that you left your share here."

"Yeah, I guess I did do that."

Zelda laughed fully now. "Tyler you know very well you did, and you do need to use that corn with your pumpkins on your porch. So, if it's convenient, I'll bring the corn out and help you decorate your front porch, give it the woman's touch. If that's all right, of course."

"All right?—it's ideal! Actually that's the reason I called. I wanted you to come out this afternoon and we'd fix up my house and then I'd charcoal steaks for us. Is it a deal?"

"You bet. I'll be out in about an hour and a half."

"That's super. I'll be at the south paddock with Dream Maker. Come down there and get me when you arrive, or if you'd rather not walk down, then just lay on your car horn for a couple of minutes. I can hear that I'm sure and I'll come a running to you as fast as a derby winner in the last furlong."

His horsey simile amused her and she suppressed a giggle. "No problem, Tyler, I'll mosey on down when I get there. See you," she added, then promptly hung up.

Zelda donned her jacket again and went back outside. She loaded all the extra decorative corn into the trunk of her car, and when she'd swept the porch clear of the left over debris, she went back inside to change into a fresh pair of jeans and the new azure blue cotton knit turtleneck she'd saved for some special cool weather occasion. Maybe it was just wishful thinking, but after last night when Tyler told her all about his father and how and why he was killed, it was like a window had been thrown open. She understood now about that emotional baggage that Tyler had had to come to terms with. Because he was willing to share these feelings with her, she felt their relationship had deepened. They had drawn closer to each other in some indescribable way. Zelda felt a warm glow flow through her knowing nothing could be more special than that.

Forty minutes later she was driving through the country-side on her way to Tyler's farm. The October wind was causing the leaves to fall in a shower of crimson, bronze, and gold. They made a paisley pattern on the ground where they fell. In a happy mood, Zelda hummed along with the music on her car radio which appropriately at the moment had on a Nat King Cole recording of *Autumn Leaves.*

When Zelda arrived at the horse farm, she parked her car at Tyler's house and headed off to find him. She'd gotten there a bit earlier than she'd told him, so she walked at a leisurely pace, and even paused a minute to admire the mounds of bright yellow chrysanthemums around Martha's house.

She walked on slowly and in a brief time she caught sight of Tyler in the distance. For some reason she couldn't explain, her heart suddenly raced, it skipped and staggered, causing her to hear the rapid pulse in her ears. As-soon as she got close enough, she called out and raised her hand in the air to wave at him. He started out at a lope to come to meet her and she quickened her steps.

As they neared each neared each other, Tyler held out his arms to her, and it seemed the most natural thing in the world for her to run into his waiting embrace. His strong arms enfolded her so that from shoulder to hip she was pressed close against him. Then he kissed her in a slow, loving way that made her totally pliant in his arms.

When Tyler released her, he cupped her face in his hands, his caressing eyes melting into hers. "I'm so glad you came out today."

"I—I gathered that," she murmured tremulously, still feeling the warmth of his kiss on her lips.

"When I saw you coming down here to the pasture to meet me just now, all I could think of was how wonderful it would be if that could happen every day." His eyes probed hers as he added. "How would you feel about that?"

"I don't think my work schedule would permit every day. Would you settle for every Sunday?" She asked, attempting to put a light note into her voice.

"No, I can't settle for that, and I'm hoping that you want much more than that too." Tyler's voice was uncompromising yet oddly gentle. His face was inches from hers. She felt the warmth of his breath on her skin and saw the smile die in his eyes and desire kindle in its place. "Can't you understand. I'm in love with you—totally and completely in love with you."

"Oh, Tyler. I had so hoped you were," she said, elation sounding in her voice.

"You knew I was. I've told you that before." He sounded surprised that she could have questioned it.

She smiled. "But never in those all-inclusive words."

"I've even more words to say than those. I want to tell you that you're like no one I've ever known. You're so understanding, sensitive, and caring. You share my hopes and dreams with me and I love you for all of that. You make me feel happy all the time I'm with you and I want you to share my life now and for always."

She could scarcely think for the thudding of her heart and the wild happiness surging through her. Her hands crept around Tyler's neck, her fingers sliding into the thickness of his hair. "I love you, Tyler. I truly love every last thing about you." It was an unconscious release of the limitless joy that now filled her heart.

He gently kissed her upturned face. "I'd say that sums it all up pretty well. We're a perfect pair and we're destined to live happily ever after. Don't you agree?" he asked, a smile wreathing his face.

She smiled too. "I have no reservations about it at all."

"Well then, there's just one more thing. You remember that you owe me one answer to a question, don't you? You promised me that, if you recall."

"Yeah, I did. But you didn't have a question for me then."

He gave her a curious, slightly amused look. "Well, I do now."

She eyed him quizzically. "Okay, what is it?"

"It's something I'd really get a charge out of knowing. I'm really curious to know what you are going to tell Mathew Redmond when he asks why a sharp, beautiful girl like you would marry a guy like me?"

"Oh, that's easy darling," she answered, her eyes twinkling with merriment. "I'll just tell him no girl in her right mind could turn down a man who's all heart, especially when he owns a thoroughbred horse that just might win the Kentucky Derby."

Tyler burst out laughing and hugged her to him. "You know, one thing about you business types, you certainly do have the right answer for everything!"